Copyright Notice

Author's Note

If you are sensitive to topics such as police brutality, social injustice, racism in America, etc, this is a fair warning that this may not be the book for you.

It happens all too often; you hear about a police officer abusing their power; whether it be brutality, shouting racial slurs, or shooting and killing an unarmed person. The majority of these cases involve a White police officer and a Black civilian, but how often is it that you hear about the roles being reversed; a Black cop shooting and killing a White person?

Would it be considered justified in the eyes of America? What about the law? I decided to take on this topic only because the opposing situation happens way too frequently, and there needs to be a conversation about this. I want to be the one to spark the much-needed conversation in this country… no, the world.

I'm not saying this book is going to change the world, but if I can at least spark a conversation, mission accomplished.

Dedication

I truly want to say thank you for supporting me on this journey. It has been nothing short of amazing; I love telling stories and writing is one of my passions, so I have to keep going and pushing the limit. This piece touches on sensitive topics, so I'm prepared for the pushback; this book may not be for everyone, and that's okay. I just hope it brings some awareness to what's going on.

I dedicate this piece to all of my fans, as well as anyone who may have ever experienced police brutality or have (or have had) family members that have fallen victim to this treatment. I don't expect this to bring you closure, but I hope this brings some awareness and sparks a much-needed conversation. I greatly appreciate your love and support, as it is what motivates me. So many things inspired me to write this piece, including the thought of releasing another work to satisfy you all, my fans. I would like to take a moment out to thank my family and friends for their consistent words of motivation, as those play major factors in me moving forward.

As you read this new piece, I ask that you read it, as though you've never known who B.M.Gage is; as though you've never heard my voice before; as though you've never listened to my show and have no idea how I think. Take a moment and learn more about me by following my Facebook page (facebook.com/officialbmgage) and my Twitter (twitter.com/officialbmgage) or my website, bmgage.com.

1

The piercing sound of an alarm awoke Christian.
Christian rolled over and pressed snooze on his phone.
He rolled back over and closed his eyes.
"Come on babe, it's time to wake up," his wife patted him.
"5 more minutes, babe," he replied as he pulled the covers over himself.

This was not going to be an easy task and she knew it.
"Come on, Christian," she pulled the covers off of him and revealed him
curled in a fetal position.
Christian extended his arms and legs fully and groaned.
"City waits for no one. Let's go, babe," his wife mentioned as she opened
the blinds, revealing the bright Florida sun.
"Keisha, I'm tired," he laughed lightly.
"Well, you should have thought about that before you decided you wanted
twenty rounds last night," Keisha laughed.
"You're definitely over-exaggerating," Christian spoke as he sat upon the
edge of the bed.
Keisha walked over to the bed and kissed him.
"Good morning, sleepyhead. I've made your breakfast."

Christian smelled the aroma of pancakes, eggs, and sausages coming from the kitchen.

"It smells delicious," he responded.

Christian looked at the time and rose to his feet.

"Ugh," he groaned again. "Do I have to go to work today?"

"You're the sergeant," Keisha laughed as she looked in the mirror. "If you don't go in, who's going to keep these streets clean?" she parted her hair and combed it.

"My superintendent," Christian smirked as he rose to his feet and walked behind Keisha.

He put his hands around her waist and kissed her on the cheek.

"Your food's going to get cold," Keisha chuckled as she dropped the comb and interlocked their fingers. "Eat first, and then you can shower and do all that," Keisha faced her husband. "I've ironed your clothes and put all of your gear together," she gave him a quick kiss on the lips.

"What did I do to deserve you?" Christian looked at her in awe.

"You were Christian Tate," she replied with a smile. "Now come on. Let's go eat," she took his hand and led him down the stairs.

Keisha and Christian walked to the kitchen and he sat down in front of the plate of food.

Keisha sat across from him and picked up her cup of coffee.

"Do you have anything special planned at work, babe?"

"Not today," Christian replied. "We don't have many open cases assigned to my department, so we're pretty much ensuring things are going the way they're supposed to."

"Make sure you let me know if something comes up," Keisha replied as she sipped her coffee.'

"I got you, babe," Christian spoke as he cut his pancakes.

The two of them listened to the news as a breaking news story came across the screen.

"Welcome back to Local 10 news. We come at you with breaking news. The officer who shot and killed Sterling Wallace has been acquitted of all charges. Thomas Nanos was patrolling the neighborhood when he saw,

what he claims, was a suspicious character walking around. He called in to report his suspicions and was advised to observe from afar and additional officers would be reporting to his location. Nanos, however, ignored the instruction and approached Wallace. A scuffle ensued and Nanos states that Wallace tried to stab him in the chest, and he was able to push Wallace off of him. He pulled out his firearm and fired the deadly shot. When other officers arrived on the scene, there was no knife discovered on Wallace."
Christian shook his head.
"It's shit like this that makes me not even want to be a cop," he spoke.
Keisha reached over and touched his hand.

"Wallace was 19 years old. With the news of the verdict being released, many are expressing outrage, and many protests are expected to take place. Which we can only imagine is going to mess with traffic, right Stormy?"
the news switched over to the traffic reporter and Keisha turned off the television.

"I guess that's what I'm up to today," Christian chuckled as he took a bite of the eggs. "It's going to be a busy day; I feel it now," he sipped his coffee.
Keisha was in shock.
"That grown man shot and killed that young boy. Now his parents are left to grieve while he walks free," she spoke. "Another case of showing what America is really capable of."
Christian didn't speak.
"Another White man kills a Black man, and he just gets a slap on the wrist."
Christian remained silent.

He knew the justice system was flawed, which is precisely why he wanted to be a police officer. He wanted to bring change and make a difference, but regardless of what he wanted to do, the change has to come from the inhabitants.
After moments of silence, Christian spoke.

"I gotta go get ready, babe," he uttered. "Breakfast was delicious," he finished the last of his coffee.

"Go on, baby," Keisha changed the television channels.

Christian kissed her on the cheek before walking to the lavatory.

Christian removed his shirt and looked in the mirror.

He admired his reflection.

Christian stood at 6 feet 2 inches and had a tightly packed body. He had a clean cut and shave, yet he felt bad.

He was part of a flawed system and there wasn't much of a change he could bring to the city.

Even though he was a black man who experienced the same struggles as his neighbors, family, and friends, he was looked at as the enemy because of the reputation of the police.

Christian got in the shower and prepared for the day.

Once Christian finished showering and getting dressed, he walked over to Keisha, who had tears in her eyes.

"Baby, it will be okay," he assured her.

"It just makes me worry about you," she spoke. "I'm even scared to have a child in this world."

"Well, I'm going to make a difference," Christian spoke, followed by a kiss on the lips. "I love you," he assured Keisha.

"I love you, too," she responded.

"I gotta go, babe," he spoke.

"Be safe."

"I will. I promise," Christian grabbed his badge from the counter and walked to the door.

"Have a good day, babe," Keisha called as he exited the home.

Christian inhaled the fresh air and listened to the sounds of the birds chirping.

It was quict on his block, but he had a feeling it wouldn't remain that way.

Christian walked to his vehicle and got inside.

He turned on his music before driving away from his home and to the police station.

***

"Miami Police Department: Seargeant Tate speaking," Christian answered his phone.

A woman was screaming in his ear on the other end.

"Mam, calm down," he spoke as he typed her number into the system. "Tell me what's going on."

"I have been transferred to you because I have a gang of people outside of my building and they're protesting the Wallace verdict," the woman spoke. "I believe the justice system has done an excellent job—."

Christian cut her off.

"Mam, the people are entitled to peacefully protest if that's what they feel…"

The woman cut him off.

"I don't think this is going to be a peaceful protest," she proclaimed. "I just need you all to come down here and establish a presence."

Christian sighed silently.

"Mam, what's your location?"

"I'm at *Chaining Day*. The jewelry store located along the strip of Miami Beach."

"Okay, and what's your name?" he asked.

"Joy Smith," she answered.

"Okay Miss Smith, we'll be right over to take a look at this. Okay?"

Christian forced himself to say this.

"Thank you," Joy spoke before hanging up.

Christian rose from his chair and grabbed his keys.

"Another complaint about nothing," he spoke to himself.

He exited his office.

"Guys, I'll be back. We got a call about protestors outside of *Chaining Day*."

"That store on the strip of Miami Beach?" an officer asked.

"That's the one."

"Don't people have a right to peacefully protest?" another officer questioned.

"They do," Christian started, "but once we get a call, we have to report and see what's going on." He shrugged his shoulders. "It's probably not even going to lead to any citations or arrests, but we gotta respond to the call."

"I'll ride with you," a female officer volunteered. "It'll get me out of this congested office," she chuckled.

"Meet me at squad car 5401," Christian spoke. "I don't think things will get out of hand, but I need some units on standby in case I make the call for backup."

"Always ready," a fourth officer replied.

"Good, Officer Gaines," Christian added. "Before I go, I just want to say how proud I am of this team. You all go above and beyond for this city, always, and even though we may be bombarded with calls regarding protests around the city today, I know we can handle it." He gave his team a pep-talk.

"We're ready for anything."

"That's what I like to hear. Keep up the good work," Christian replied before walking out the door.

He walked to the police car and sat inside. He adjusted the volume of the police scanner and waited for his ride-along.

She got in the passenger's seat and put on her seatbelt.

"You ready to go, Frankie?" he asked.

"Ready to do nothing? Sure," she chuckled.

"You're right about that," Christian laughed. "But, we gotta respond."

Christian left the lot with no lights or siren.

He drove to the location of the protestors and parked the car.

"They're in the middle of the strip, so we gotta park down here," he spoke as he opened the driver's door.

Frankie opened the passenger's door and walked around.

They both ensured their weapons were secure and approached the protestors.

"No justice, no peace," the crowd chanted.

Many of the protesters held up signs as well. They were blocking the entrance to the stores.

"I'm assuming they just want a police presence," Christian spoke to Frankie.

"It's a peaceful protest," she uttered. "I don't see what the issue is."

One of the protestors saw Christian and Frankie and commented.

"Oh, look, it's the police."

The rest of the protestors jeered at this comment.

"You're gonna shoot me for protesting?" the protestor wore a hood and shouted in Christian's face.

Christian knew it was best to remain silent.

"Hell no, we won't go," the protester shouted in his face. "Hell no, we won't go," he started the chant.

"Officer Banks, please go into the store and retrieve Joy," Christian spoke to Frankie.

"You good out here?" she asked.

"I'm fine. Go on," Christian stressed.

Frankie walked inside the store and the protestors continued to shout in his face.

"You can't arrest me for protesting peacefully. Pig!"

"And to make it worse, it's a black man that's here to stop us from protesting," the leader shouted with a laugh. "Talk about an Uncle Tom."

"Guys, I'm not here to break up your peaceful demonstration," Christian finally spoke. "I was called to the scene—."

"Bullshit!" the leader shouted. "No justice, no peace."

The crowd chanted with the leader.

Frankie returned outside with Joy.

"Miss Smith, I am Sergeant Tate. We spoke over the phone," Christian extended his hand for a shake.

"Save that shit," she exclaimed. "These hoodlums are preventing my business from thriving."

"Hoodlums?!" The leader shouted. "You better watch it!"
"You're a damn animal," Joy screamed.

Frankie stood in between Joy and the protestors.
"Miss Smith, I'm going to need for you to calm down," Christian warned.
"Or what?" she asked. "Do your job and arrest these bastards. And then people wonder why I said the justice system did their job with the Wallace case."
"Joy, that's enough," Christian raised his tone.
"We will no longer be a victim," the leader spoke over the bullhorn.
"America with three 'k's has been killing our people for hundreds of years now, and we've just succumbed to it. No longer shall we be oppressed," the leader shouted.

Joy reached over and attempted to hit one of the protestors, but failed since Frankie and Christian were in front of her.
The noise level increased as the situation was quickly getting out of hand.
Christian quickly turned Joy around and put her hands behind her back.
"What the hell?" she asked as he put his handcuffs on her.
"They have the right to protest; you don't have the right to hit anyone," Christian explained as he walked her to the car.
Protestors cheered as Christian and Frankie walked to the vehicle.
"How does that shit feel?" the leader shouted to Joy.
"Go to hell!" she retaliated. "Thank God that Nanos got one of you filthy demons off the street."

Hearing how Joy was speaking was irritating Christian but he didn't show his frustration at her racist comments.
"Joy Smith, you are under arrest. You have the right to remain silent, anything you say can and will be used against you in the court of law," Christian read her the Miranda rights while putting her in the back of his car.
"Frankie, stay over here with her. I'm going to make sure these protestors stay in line," Christian walked back over to the protestors.

What used to be jeers and insults towards Christian were now slight cheers. "We're about to take her down to the station," he spoke to the leader of the pack. "But do me a favor," Christian spoke.
The leader raised his eyebrows.
"Keep this protest peaceful," Christian handed the man his card and walked away.

2

"How was work, babe?" Keisha asked as she sat on the bed.

"Work was work," Christian chuckled as he unbuttoned his shirt. "We had to make 20 arrests today," he shook his head.

"All because of the verdict?" she questioned.

"Yep," Christian uttered. "None of our arrests were Black either. A good number of them were business owners or White civilians who called the police, but then chose to make a stupid decision," Christian removed his watch. "It felt good to see our people peacefully protesting this instead of causing riots."

"Well, that's only here. Other parts of the country are going berzerk," Keisha chuckled.

"This is only the beginning," Christian replied as he walked over to the bed and sat down next to Keisha.

Keisha put her hands on top of Christian's.

"We can only pray, babe," she kissed him on the cheek.

"I don't know what's going on," Christian spoke as he laid down.

Keisha was silent as she laid next to her husband.

"We gotta keep our heads up," she smiled.

"When I went to the scene of a protest earlier, there was one guy who stood out to me," Christian remembered. "It felt bad to know that he looked at me as if I was the enemy," he shook his head. "But then, when I arrested the store owner for attempted battery, he applauded me. It's a shame that it's really come down to a race war."

"Babe, think about the things he may have seen in his life and then the recent killing of this young unarmed Black man by a White police officer."

"I know," Christian spoke. "And that's what made it hard for me to face him." He held Keisha's hand tightly. "I want to be seen as the hero, not the villain."

"Well, I'll always see you as my hero," Keisha spoke after a few seconds of silence.

Christian kissed her on the lips.

"And the messed up part, is that this keeps happening, and the responses are only getting worse."

***

Christian and Frankie walked inside of the supermarket to speak to the manager regarding the recent protests.

"Maria Vasquez," he started as he showed his badge. "I am Sergeant Tate, this is my partner, Officer Banks."

Christian looked to his right and made eye contact with a young boy.

The boy quickly looked away and walked off.

Christian directed his attention back to Maria.

"Hello, Sergeant Tate," Maria spoke. "I'm glad you all stopped by," she shook Christian's hand, followed by Frankie's. "We've had a few people come in the store protesting today."

"What did they look like?" Frankie asked.

"There were males and females. Black and White," she started.

Frankie jotted down the notes.

Christian raised his eyebrows.

"Teens," Maria continued. "It was an interesting mix; you had some Whites on the side with Blacks who feel that justice wasn't served, and you had some Blacks on the side with the Whites who felt that justice was served."

"So, what's going on?" Christian asked.

"Well, I'm worried," Maria spoke. "I feel like this is going to spark fights and feuds across the city."

Christian looked around at the nearby cameras in the store.

"We truly understand your concern," Frankie spoke. "And we're going to do what we can to prevent this from happening."

"Maria, are these cameras recording?" Christian asked.

"Yes, Sergeant," she answered. "I'm sure it has them on video. It was a large group of them."

"May we see them?" Christian asked.

"I can get you all a copy of the tapes," Maria asked. "Give me a second. I'll be right back."

Maria walked away and Christian continued to speak to Frankie.

"What do you think?" he asked.

"I think shit's getting out of hand," she shook her head. "And it's only going to get worse before it gets better."

"Nothing's going to change until the system is changed. And with Nanos walking free, I know this isn't going away, especially since he can't be retried for this crime. That's what people are really mad at."

Frankie paced the floor and shook her head.

"It's all about race. That's the bad part about all of this."

Regardless of how Christian felt, his position was preventing him from saying certain things.

"As long as we're not letting race affect how we do *our* jobs, that's all that matters."

Maria returned to the front of the store with a flash drive.

She passed it to Christian.

"Okay, Sergeant. This contains the footage from earlier. It starts at their entrance and goes until they exit."

"Thank you, Miss Vasquez," Christian replied. "We'll be taking this back to the station, but if they come back, do not hesitate to call me," he handed her a card.

"Thank you," she spoke.

Christian and Frankie left the store and got back in the police car.

"You ready for a riot?" Frankie chuckled.

"I'm ready for *anything*," Christian replied as he started the engine. "But I hope it doesn't escalate to that."

Christian started the drive back to the police department.

"Frankie, did you see the young man back at the store? He was wearing a 'Make America Great Again' hat."

"I think I missed him," Frankie replied. "What about him?"

"I just got a weird vibe from him. When we made eye contact, he quickly looked away and ran off."

"You don't think you're being a little paranoid about it?" Frankie chuckled.

"Eh, maybe," Christian shrugged, "but so far, when I have a gut feeling about something, it's been accurate."

"You wanna double back for him?" she asked.

"Nah, but keep your ears peeled," Christian continued the drive to the station.

***

"Yeah, babe. I'll be home late tonight. They got me putting in extra hours. Rogers called in sick," Christian spoke to Keisha over the phone.

"Okay, babe. Well, I guess I'll put this food in the fridge," she responded.

"Be safe, baby," she blew Christian a kiss through the phone.

"I'll be home as soon as I can, babe. I love you."

"I love you too, baby," Keisha spoke.

Christian ended the call.

"Sergeant Tate," the dispatch called over the radio.

"Tate, here," Christian replied to the call.

"We have a call about a suspicious character over near 44th and Michigan. No visible description of the character; too dark to get a descriptive visual."
"10-4," he replied. "I'm in the area now. I'll swing by and check it out. Stand-by," Christian replied.
He turned on his siren lights and drove to the location.
"One street light is on," Christian reported.
He turned on his spotlight and shined it around the area.
"Where are you?" he spoke to himself as he looked around.
He saw a man crouched between two bushes and stepped out of the vehicle.
"What's going on?" Christian shouted.

The man quickly rose to his feet and started to run.
"Nope, not today," Christian replied as he returned to his vehicle and turned on the sound to the siren. He drove the car forward and made a U-turn at the cul-de-sac.
Christian made sure to keep an eye on the man as he ran in between the homes.
"Suspect is fleeing," Christian reported. "I'm continuing the chase on foot. Running northbound on Michigan."
Christian quickly got out of the car and chased behind the suspect.
"Miami P-D, freeze!" he shouted.
The man continued to run and Christian reached near his utility belt.
"If you don't stop, you will be tased," he warned him.
The suspect came to a fence and began to climb it.

Christian pulled out his taser and discharged it.
The charge hit the man in the back and he fell off the fence and returned to the Earth.
"Shit!" the man screamed.
Christian jogged over to the man while holding the trigger on the taser.
As he got closer, he noticed it was the young man from the supermarket.
"Why you runnin', man?" Christian asked as he approached him.
"Fuck you, man," he spoke and tried to stand to his feet.
Christian walked over and pushed the man down to the ground.
"Sit down," he chuckled.

Christian reached in his back pocket and pulled out his handcuffs.
The suspect quickly hopped to his feet and reached behind him; he pulled
out a weapon.

Christian was surprised to see how quickly the situation escalated.
The man cocked his gun to fire a shot, and Christian pulled out his weapon
and dropped the handcuffs.
"Drop your weapon," Christian ordered the man.
The suspect quickly put his gun in his waistband and ran.
"Man, oh man," Christian stated aloud. "Suspecting is fleeing again," he
spoke into his shoulder, picked up the handcuffs, and resumed the chase.

"Miami P-D!" Christian shouted as he chased the suspect.
Christian noticed as the man slid his hand into his waistband and pulled out
the weapon.
"Subject has a weapon," Christian reported. "Drop your weapon!" he
shouted.
The man was breathing heavily as he ran and prepared the weapon.
While preparing the gun, the man didn't notice the root growing from the
ground and tripped.
He fell to the floor; allowing Christian to catch up to him.
Christian pulled out his weapon and aimed it as he approached the man.
"Do not move!" he ordered. "Stay on your stomach."
Christian inched closer to the suspect.
"Let me see your hands!" Christian shouted.

The suspect turned around with his weapon loaded and aimed at Christian
and started to pull the trigger.

Christian responded to the slight movement.
Christian shot him in the chest; the man fell back to the ground.
"Shots fired," Christian reported over the radio. "Shit," he whispered to
himself.
Christian walked closer to the man with his gun aimed and bent down and
moved the weapon out of reach.

He put two fingers to the man's neck and felt a faint pulse.

"I need an EMT over here at 47th and Michigan," he spoke.

"Stay with me," Christian was frantic as he holstered his weapon.

The suspect chuckled and uttered words to Christian, but he ignored them and covered the gunshot wound with his jacket before beginning chest compressions.

"*EMTs are en route,*" the dispatch spoke.

"Breathe," Christian pleaded as he continued the compressions.

Christian wasn't thinking about anything at this point but keeping the suspect alive.

There was already an uproar surrounding a police officer shooting and killing a civilian. This happening was beyond what he could have warranted.

He soon heard sirens approaching and people opened their doors.

He heard multiple phone conversations and his radio was sounding off with calls about the situation.

"Don't you die on me," Christian spoke to the man as he continued the compressions.

The ambulance drove next to Christian and the paramedics quickly unloaded.

"How long has he been down?" the paramedic asked.

"Five minutes," Christian spoke.

His thoughts were all over the place with what had just transpired.

Additional police officers arrived on the scene, including Christian's boss.

"Sergeant Tate, are you okay?" a member from his unit asked.

The paramedics pumped fluid into the man's body and injected him with different medications.

"I'm good," Christian started. "Everything went down so quickly, I didn't even have time to call for backup. I did report everything back, including that the subject had a weapon, but I didn't have much time for anything else."

Samuel walked over and removed his sunglasses.

"Give it to me," he stated in a gruff voice.

Christian sighed.

"I responded to a call about a suspicious character about 9:45. When I arrived, a brief pursuit ensued," he started.

"Where did the pursuit start?" Samuel asked.

"It began on 44th and Michigan," he answered. "It really was a brief pursuit."

"Keep going," Samuel persisted.

"Once we came to the fence," Christian pointed in the direction of the fence, "he began to climb. By this time, I'd already had my taser out, and I discharged it. The platelet hit him and he fell to the ground. I came over to him and pulled out my handcuffs and he jumped up and drew a weapon. I ordered him to drop the weapon, and he put the firearm away. He fled. I chased behind him, where he pulled the firearm out once more while running but he tripped and fell on the root of the tree," Christian pointed to the root that he tripped over, "and it allowed me time to catch up to him. I ordered him to stay on his stomach and to show me his hands. Instead of complying, he quickly turned around and aimed the gun at me. He started to pull the trigger, so I fired mine," Christian narrated.

Christian knew this wasn't going to be easy and he knew this wasn't going away.

"Let's pray that he's going to be alright," Samuel uttered. "But what we have to do right now is head to the station and take your story down."

"You all have my back on this, right?" Christian asked for assurance.

"We're a team," Samuel spoke. "And I have faith in what you're saying, but we have to follow protocol and do things the right way."

Christian looked back and couldn't believe what had just happened.

He saw the paramedics secure the gurney in the back of the vehicle and heard them turn on their sirens.

He shook his head in frustration as he walked to his vehicle.

"Let's get a unit to trail the ambulance to the hospital," Samuel announced. "Report back with the condition of the suspect as soon as you hear something. Get additional units over here to take photos of everything. Do not touch anything until the photos are collected and the evidence is processed. Once the photography is finished, follow procedure in bringing the evidence back." He directed his attention back to Christian. "Tate, follow me back to the station," he finished.

Christian got in his vehicle and followed his supervisor out of the cul-de-sac onto the main road.

Once the two arrived back at the police station, Samuel walked into his office. Christian followed him inside the room; Samuel closed the door.

"Have a seat, Tate," he spoke.

Christian sat down in the cold chair.

He still felt numb at what had just occurred. He didn't know whether he should be fearful of the outcome or to feel positive about having a good shoot.

"I need your weapon," Samuel spoke calmly as he walked to the seat across from Christian.

He raised his eyebrows.

"It's procedure," Samuel assured him.

Christian nodded his head and reached down by his waistband. He removed the weapon and unloaded it. He cleared the bullet from the chamber.

The single bullet fell on the table and sounded as if it were a bomb being dropped.

Christian laid his weapon on the table and looked up.

Samuel couldn't make eye contact with Christian.

He knew Christian was a good cop, and he wouldn't have used his weapon if he didn't feel the need to do so.

Samuel pulled a recorder from his desk.

"I need for you to walk me through everything that occurred before the shooting," he spoke shakily.

Christian knew the procedure that had to be taken following a shooting; he'd gone through it with other officers in the past.

It was the surrounding situations that made Christian fear the outcome of this shooting.

"Around 9:45 p.m. eastern," Christian was very specific for the recording, "I got a call about a suspicious character around 44th and Michigan."
"Why were you called?" Samuel asked.
"I was out patrolling in place of Officer Rogers. He took a sick day, and I stayed behind for a few hours."
"Proceed," Samuel instructed.
"I was in the area of 44th and Michigan, so I took the call. I drove to the area, which was only illuminated with one street light and my vehicle lights, so I turned on my spotlight," Christian took a deep breath. "I shined the light over by the bushes, and I saw a man crouching. I exited my vehicle and called out to him. The man ran and I began a chase."
"And at what point did you catch up to him?"
Christian took a breath of air and continued.

"The suspect came in contact with a gate and tried climbing it. I gave him the warning to stop or he was going to get tased, but he didn't listen. I fired the taser and he was hit. He fell to the ground and I pulled out my handcuffs. I walked over to him and he leaped to his feet before pulling out a weapon." Christian remembered all of the details and obtained chills while telling this story.
"I instructed the gentleman to drop his weapon and he put it away before fleeing again. I began chase again and around 46th and Michigan, the suspect tripped over a tree root and fell to the ground. I was able to catch up to him. I instructed for him to remain on his stomach and to extend his arms. The gentleman quickly turned back around and aimed his weapon. I instructed the gentleman once more to drop his weapon. He didn't listen and adjusted his finger on the trigger. I had a choice to make and I made it. But once I shot him, I performed chest compressions; no luck."
"So, you feared for your life?" Samuel asked.
"Yes."

3

Christian walked into his home and didn't remove any of his clothing. The recollection of events continuously replayed in his mind.
He walked to his bedroom and crawled in bed next to Keisha.
He wrapped his arms around her and kissed her on the cheek.
She felt his body around hers and slowly awoke from her sleep.
She turned and faced Christian.
"Hey babe," Keisha spoke softly.
"Hey baby," Christian replied dryly.

Keisha could tell that something was bothering him.
"What's wrong?" she asked.
Christian let out a sigh.
"Let's talk about it in the morning babe," Christian replied.
Keisha rubbed her husband's chest and kissed him on the cheek.
She could feel his heart was beating quickly.
"No," she insisted. "Tell me what's going on."
Keisha rubbed her eyes as Christian sighed.
"I shot a suspect today," he spoke.

Keisha put her hand over her mouth.

"Oh my God, babe, are you okay?" she embraced him.

"I'm fine," he started. "But my job may not be."

Keisha raised an eyebrow.

"What do you mean, babe?"

"I.A.D. is conducting an investigation, babe," Christian's voice was shaky. "It was a clean shot, but you know how these things are." He remained vague.

"Babe…" Keisha started.

"He pulled out a gun on me, babe," Christian explained. "I had to make a decision: either he went home tonight or I did."

Keisha rubbed his chest and kissed his cheek.

"Everything will be alright," she assured him.

Christian and Keisha went to sleep shortly after the conversation.

The next morning, once Christian was dressed, Keisha walked up to him.

"It seems so weird seeing you without your gun on your waist," she chuckled, as she tried to keep a comforting tone.

"It feels weird, too," Christian added. "I'll be glad when they close the investigation. I'm being questioned by I.A.D. today."

"Are you ready for it?" Keisha questioned.

"Yeah babe," Christian spoke with uncertainty but did his best to sound confident. "I mean, it was a clean shot and I did everything by the books, so it should be fine."

Keisha kissed him on the lips.

"Make sure they understand that my man is not a killer and he's one of the most dedicated and faithful officers there is."

"As long as I know and my baby knows, that's all that matters," Christian embraced her. "My thing is what the media is going to make of this," he slightly shook his head.

"It's hilarious," she spoke, "because you hear about this all the time."

"Yeah, but not in this scenario. And it only makes it worse because the country is in an uproar over the Wallace case. And trust me; I understand their frustration," Christian glanced at the clock. "I'm a Black man in

America, and our children are going to be Black, and if that shit happens to them, I swear it's going to be hell on Earth."

Keisha noticed him glancing at the clock.
"Babe, let's not focus on that for now," she gave him a quick kiss on the lips. "Don't be late, and make sure those bastards know that that shit was justified."
Keisha walked to the kitchen and grabbed Christian's lunch bag.
"I got you, babe," he spoke as Keisha passed him the bag. "I love you," he walked out of the door and felt his pocket for his keys.
"I love you, too, baby. Try to have a good day at work."
Keisha closed the door and Christian walked to his car.

He started the vehicle and turned on some music before driving away.
Although music was playing from his speakers, he felt as though it was nothing but silence around him.
He'd used his weapon before but never killed anyone with it.
But the murder wasn't messing with his head; he was more concerned with his image in the police force as well as the media.
Beads of sweat formed across Christian's forehead as he veered closer to the station.
He pulled into the parking lot.
"Ready or not," he whispered to himself as he exited the vehicle.

Christian entered the police station, and it seemed as though all eyes immediately focused on him.
Christian held his head high as he walked to his office.
He sat in his chair and felt naked without his firearm and handcuffs.
Christian sat at his desk with his hands interlocked as he looked at his locked computer screen.
He was mentally preparing himself for his interrogation, as he knew that they weren't going to make it easy for him.
Moments later, there was a knock at his door.
"Tate, come with me," Samuel spoke as he poked his head inside.
Christian rose from his chair and followed his supervisor out of the door.

As Christian exited his office, he couldn't help but feel like all eyes were still watching him.

"Tate, now I.A.D is going to ask you questions from all angles," he spoke.

"I'm familiar with the process, Sam," Christian spoke.

The two entered the room and found six board members sitting at a table. Samuel patted Christian's shoulder and Christian sat down across from the members.

Samuel sat next to Christian and a member pulled out a recorder.

Christian noticed the omnidirectional microphone placed in the center of the table. He was all too familiar with the setup from when he would enter the room with officers on his squad.

The head of the department pulled out a tape recorder and pressed record.

"I am Lieutenant Leonard Buckingham sitting here alongside Sergeant Pamela James, D.A. Angela Martin, Sergeant Gregory Williams, Sergeant Lucille Beckham, and Officer Patrick McGregory. It is now ten hundred hours on the 3rd of March, 2019, and we are questioning Sergeant Christian Tate on the shooting death of 18-year-old Benjamin Smith."

That was the first time Christian heard the age and name of the suspect.

"*Shit,*" he thought.

"Sergeant Tate, we're going to ask you to walk us through what occurred yesterday, and from there, we will ask you a series of questions. I know you know the reason for the questioning, but we're just determining whether or not it was a justified shoot and where you were mentally at the time of the shooting."

Christian nodded his head in approval.

"Please state your name and rank for the record," Leonard spoke.

"Sergeant Christian Tate," Christian answered.

He knew it would be best to keep the answers short and to the point.

"D.A. Angela Martin," Angela announced for the microphone, "Sergeant Tate, walk us through the events leading up to the shooting yesterday," Angela spoke.
Christian sat tall and showed no sign of defeat. He knew they would take the fear and run with it.

"At approximately 9:45 last night, I received a call of a suspicious character around 44th and Michigan. I responded to the call and drove to the scene, where I saw a character crouched between two bushes. I called out to him and got his attention," Christian remembered, "and from there, he ran and I began a pursuit."
"Sergeant Lucille Beckham. Sergeant Tate, why did he run?" Lucille asked.
"I don't know," Christian replied, "and at the time, I was just concerned with detaining him."
"Why?" Lucille asked again.
"Protocol is to detain the suspect," Christian replied, not giving Lucille the satisfaction of knowing he was getting irate.
"Continue," Leonard spoke.
"The suspect came to a gate and tried climbing it. I announced the warning that he would be tased, but he didn't listen. I discharged the taser and it struck him in the back. He fell to the ground and I pulled out my handcuffs," Christian kept his story consistent, as he knew they would review the recording with Samuel from the previous night. "As I approached the suspect, he jumped to his feet and pulled out a weapon and smirked at me. I instructed him to drop his weapon," Christian inhaled.
"And what happened next?" Angela asked.
"He returned his weapon to his waistband and continued to flee."
"Go on," Angela spoke.
"He ran for a few more feet before he tripped and fell over a tree's root. When he fell, it allowed me just enough time to catch up," Christian inhaled sharply. "When I caught up with him, I instructed him to remain flat on his stomach with his arms extended so his hands were visible. He flipped around and he pulled out his weapon once more. I instructed him to drop his weapon, but this time, he didn't listen," Christian continued. "He

adjusted his finger on the trigger and prepared to shoot. I think it's obvious what happened next," Christian spoke.

The panel looked at each other.

Christian sighed and continued.

"Once I shot him, I did perform chest compressions, but to no avail."

"So, you did try to perform C.P.R. on the deceased Smith?"

"My intention wasn't to kill anyone," Christian defended. "I wanted to disorient the suspect so that I could make it home to my wife."

"And tasing him couldn't do the job?" Angela asked.

"The suspect pulled out a gun when I approached him. The taser didn't have much of an effect on him."

"You just said you wanted to make it home to your wife. Well, Benjamin Smith had a mother at home waiting on him. Did you care if he made it home?"

"Of course I cared," Christian slightly raised his tone. "I've worked my ass off to protect this city and with all of the years I've put into my work, it shouldn't even be a question whether or not my intentions were pure," he shook his head. "I do not come to work for that reason."

"Yeah, but a few weeks ago, during the Wallace trial, you were overheard by a fellow officer saying how you hope it was a positive outcome because quote 'you're tired of your people getting killed and there being no repercussions'. End quote." Angela read off a piece of paper.

Christian chuckled.

"No, no, no. This is *not* about race," he assured them.

"Explain what you meant," Leonard spoke.

Christian looked at Samuel before proceeding.

"It's 2019," he spoke. "I was just making an honest observation about how things go in terms of police brutality versus the civilians."

"So, with Officer Nanos receiving a 'not guilty' verdict, do you believe that justice was served?" Angela asked.

"And if not, is that why you killed Smith yesterday?" Leonard added.

Christian scoffed.

"First of all, my beliefs about the trial have absolutely nothing to do with how I do my job or what transpired yesterday. I come in day in and day out to protect the city and keep the streets clean, that's it. And with me not having a shooting on my record in the past 5 years, that's got to count for something," he explained.

Lucille took notes on Christian's behavior and responses.
"Lieutenant Miller," Angela spoke to Samuel, "I think we need to speak to you in private regarding your staff sergeant, Sergeant Tate."
Angela looked at Christian.
"Sergeant Tate, if you haven't already done so, please surrender your weapons and handcuffs to Lieutenant Miller at this time."
"Lieutenant Samuel Miller," Samuel announced for the recorder and camera. "They've already been surrendered," Samuel spoke. "They are locked in a drawer in my office."
"Perfect," Angela spoke.
All of the board members looked at each other and gave a slight nod, as to say that they reached a decision telepathically.

"Sergeant Christian Tate, we are placing you on administrative leave while this shooting is being investigated," Leonard spoke. "During this time, you are *not* allowed to be…"
Christian was furious and didn't allow Leonard to finish.
"I know how this works," he interrupted. "Are we done here?" Christian asked as he rose to his feet.
"Your administrative leave is effective immediately. Lieutenant Miller, please have an officer escort Christian from the building."
Christian pulled out his badge and key-card and placed it on the table.
"I'll walk him out," Samuel spoke.
Samuel rose to his feet with Christian and they left the room.

"Tate, I'm sorry," Samuel spoke as they walked to the front.
"But not sorry enough to defend me. Got it," Christian shook his head.
"Got it."
Samuel shook his head as they reached the front door.

"I'll be in touch, Tate," he spoke.

Christian opened the door and, to no surprise, he saw news vans outside with reporters all around.

"You got this," he whispered to himself as he walked down the steps.

"Sergeant Tate," many reporters called out as they ran over to him.

One woman made her way to the front.

"Sergeant Tate, I'm Rebecca Stanton with Channel 5 News. Any word on the shooting death of Benjamin Smith yesterday? What provoked it?"

"The case is undergoing an investigation. I am not permitted to discuss those details at the time," Christian replied.

"But can you confirm that you were the shooter who fired the deadly shot?" Rebecca asked.

"How could you kill an innocent child?" A pedestrian asked before he could answer Rebecca.

Christian made eye contact with the pedestrian.

"Innocent?!" he questioned aloud.

Christian had to quickly regain his composure and turned away.

"No further comments," he spoke as he walked to his car.

The reporters continued to call out his name and followed him.

Christian climbed into his car and drove away.

***

Later that evening, Christian and Keisha were sitting at the table discussing the day's events and were watching the news.

"*Tonight, we have the family of Benjamin Smith here with us,*" the reporter spoke. "*Smith is the 18-year-old who was shot and killed by Sergeant Tate of the Miami Police Department. Thank you all for being here with us this evening.*"

"*Thank you for having us,*" the male spoke.

"*Mr. Smith, can you tell us about your son?*"

"*My son was a good child,*" his father spoke as Benajmin's mother began to cry.

The news displayed a small image of Benjamin in the corner. He was wearing a suit and smiling.

"Raised in a two parent household, was on the Dean's List, and was majoring in business. He was set to graduate in June. He always had his head on straight, so for him to be murdered by a police officer last night has us baffled," his father spoke.

"Mrs. Smith," the reporter started, *"it's reported that your son pulled out a .22 caliber handgun on Sergeant Tate yesterday, which is why Tate fired his weapon."*

"I call B.S. on that," the mother spoke in between tears, *"but I'm not here to tear the man who killed my son down. May God bless his soul; his guilt will do the job. But, we do want justice for our son."*

Christian turned off the television.

"The shit starts," he scoffed.

"Baby, you've gotta keep your head," Keisha pleaded.

Christian rose to his feet and grabbed a glass from the cabinet.

"Administrative leave, and now this," he filled the glass with ice water. "I wonder what these people consider justice."

Keisha was silent.

"I damn near get killed, but I'm the bad guy for saving my life. Yes, they have a dead child, but I took the right actions."

Keisha stood and walked over to Christian.

She put her hands around his waist and laid her head on his back.

Christian turned around and embraced Keisha.

"It will be okay," she tried to comfort him. "Your team will back you up; that should be a given."

"It should be," Christian sipped the water, "But you know that Sam didn't even do anything to defend me when I.A.D was questioning me? I've been on his team for the past eight years, and he knows my character."

Keisha hated seeing her husband in this state.

Christian seemed as if he was defeated, and that wasn't the man she knew.

"You know what you will have to do?" Keisha asked.

"What's that?" Christian asked.

"Stop worrying about this damn case and go fix us some dinner," she tried to get a laugh out of him.

"Nah, babe," Christian smiled. "I think I'm just going to lay down," he walked to the stairs and seemed to disappear.
"I'll be up in a second, babe," Keisha called to him.

Christian didn't reply. He didn't know how he was going to deal with the pressure from the media and the police department about this shooting. He turned on the television and sat down.

"*We are starting a petition that demands that Sergeant Tate be reprimanded for his actions,*" the mother of the deceased spoke.
"Yep, it starts," Christian mumbled to himself.
He watched the images move across the screen of the child and noticed the images the media chose to select to represent him.

"Look at this shit," he spoke aloud. "Graduation gowns, diplomas, volunteering; but let it be my people, they will dig deep to find a picture of us raising our middle fingers to the camera," he referenced the media's tactics and how they handled the Sterling Wallace case. "*This young man went to the store after school and returned on a slab in the coroner's office,*" the reporter spoke.

Christian paced the floor; all he could do was wait and see what was going to happen.

4

Christian sat at the kitchen table with Keisha and was eating breakfast. A week had passed since the shooting and Christian was still on administrative leave.

"Have you heard anything else regarding the shooting?" Keisha asked after taking a sip of the orange juice.

"I haven't heard a thing," Christian spoke. "I wish they'd hurry with this investigation," Christian spoke. "It was a good shoot and everything was done by the books," he shook his head. "I even performed C.P.R. on the kid. If I didn't care, I wouldn't have done any of that."

"Babe, I know where your heart lies," Keisha spoke calmly. "And your boss should also know that what you're telling him is the truth." Christian nodded in agreement.

"He *should*," he uttered.

Christian thought about how the media was having a field day with the shooting and were showing the most innocent images of the victim that they could find; but let it had been someone of his caliber, they'd dig deep to try to blame the victim for his own death.

Christian continued eating his breakfast when there was a knock at the door.

He rose to his feet and walked to the door.

"Who is it, babe?" Keisha asked as he reached the door.

"I'm not sure, babe," Christian spoke as he tried to see through the viewport, but it was covered.

He unlocked the door and opened it.

"Hey Sam," Christian started and saw numerous officers behind Samuel. Christian's slight enthusiasm left his body after seeing the other officers.

"Christian Tate," one of the officers spoke as he came to the front.

Christian looked at the officer.

"Yes?" Christian asked.

"You are under arrest for the murder of Benjamin Smith," the officer reached for Christian's arm.

Christian's heart sunk to his stomach as he heard this, but he didn't show weakness.

"No!" Keisha shouted as she stood behind Christian.

He moved his arm so that the officer couldn't get a grip on it; not to show aggression, but because he couldn't believe what was happening.

"Give me a moment," Christian spoke.

Christian turned and faced Keisha. Her face was puffy and her eyes had tears coming from them.

He kissed her on the lips before speaking.

"Babe, call my lawyer," Christian spoke. "And be strong for me; I will be fine," he forced a smile.

"I love you, baby," Keisha embraced him tightly and kissed him.

Christian returned the embrace and kiss.

"I love you, too," Christian replied. "Hold it down for me, babe," he uttered.

"Come on," Samuel whispered to Christian.

Christian let go of Keisha and put his hands behind his back.

"Christian Tate, you have the right to remain silent. Anything you say can and will be used against you in the court of law," the officer recited as he locked the handcuffs.

He led Christian out of the room.

"He will be okay," Samuel spoke to Keisha. "I'll be in touch with you about what's going on." He patted her on the shoulder and all she could do was glare at him.

Christian's thoughts were racing as the officers walked him down the steps of his home.

The officer opened the door and they were greeted by reporters and cameras.

"Sergeant Tate, over here," a woman shouted as she ran to Christian and pointed the microphone in his face.

Christian kept his head down as he was escorted to the police vehicle.

"Do you have any word on the shooting death of Mr. Smith?" a different reporter asked.

Numerous cameramen were taking images of the police walking Christian to the car.

"No comment," Samuel spoke to the reporters,

The arresting officer placed Christian in the back of his vehicle and closed the door.

Christian didn't want to look up; he kept his head low during the commute to the police station.

Keisha hung up the phone with the lawyer and turned on the television for sound.

She paced around the home looking for her checkbook; she knew she would need it.

"*This just in, Sergeant Christian Tate has been arrested and charged with the murder of 18-year-old, Benjamin Smith.*"

The camera showed a video of Christian being escorted into the police station.

Keisha's eyes filled with tears once again as she looked at the television.

"*The arrest comes after the public outcry demanding an arrest be made. Joining us now are the parents of Mr. Smith. Theresa, Benard, welcome to the show,*" the host welcomed the parents.

The camera focused on the parents.

"*How do you all feel now since Christian Tate was arrested: the man who shot your son?*"

The mom wiped her eyes.

"*It doesn't bring my son back,*" she began, "*but it's a start. The justice system works,*" she finished.

"Bullshit," Keisha spoke before rising to her feet.

"*Many people feel that he was only arrested due to the public outcry and he will be back on the streets in a number of days,*" the host added.

"*Forget what they're saying,*" the father added. "*Personally, we feel that justice was served, so we're taking it a day at a time.*"

But Keisha had a completely different feeling as the tears flowed from her face. She did feel bad that they'd lost a child, but she knew that Christian didn't just shoot Benjamin because he wanted to shoot someone.

She turned off the television and rose to her feet.

Keisha turned her head to the left and saw an image of her and Christian in uniform.

"I know you wouldn't do something like this out of spite or anger," she spoke to the picture. "I will figure something out," she uttered as she walked out of the home.

***

Christian looked around the holding cell as he shook his head.

He couldn't believe that he was inside of a holding cell as a prisoner.

The officer put Christian in his own holding cell for his own safety.

"Can I get my phone call?" Christian spoke through the bars.

"You'll get it," the male officer called out; never turning around to look at him.

Christian slammed his hands against the bars and sat on the bench.

"When is my court date?" Christian asked.

"Christian," another officer approached the cell. "The best thing for you to do right now is to remain calm," she spoke, "and stop speaking so much," she whispered and nodded to the numerous cameras and microphones. "There have been so many threats that we had each of the cells bugged," she whispered.

Christian nodded his head in agreement.

"Sergeant Tate," the officer spoke, "your first court date is in two days," she calmly replied.

She unlocked the cell and touched Christian on the shoulder.

Christian followed her from the cell to the phones.

"Let's make it quick before they realize that you're gone," she hurried Christian.

He picked up the phone and called his lawyer.

"This is Andrew," he answered.

"Drew, this is Christian," he spoke in a low tone.

"Hey Chris, what's going on?" Andrew asked.

"Not good," Christian replied. "I need for you to come to the jail. I've been arrested."

Andrew put his keys in his pocket.

"Okay, I'm on my way now," he replied. "You already know the rules," Andrew finished.

"I'm at the 8th district," Christian added.

"I'll be there soon," Andrew spoke. "Keep your head."

"See you soon," Christian spoke before he hung up.

The lady officer looked at Christian.

"Can I make one more call?" he pleaded.

"To whom?" she asked.

"I want to call my wife so that she knows what's going on."

The officer agreed and Christian called Keisha.

Christian dialed Keisha's number and she answered on the first ring.

"Hello?"

"Babe, it's me," Christian responded. "Drew is about to come down here and speak to me; they have me in a holding cell by myself; maximum security."

"Okay babe, so what do you need from me?" she asked.

"Babe, keep your eye on the media. I know how that sounds, but I need to know what's going on," Christian knew the news would have more insight than what he would receive while on the inside. "Also, babe, keep the checkbook close."

Keisha sniffled.

"And don't cry," Christian chuckled. "I'm going to be okay."

Hearing Christian's voice telling her not to cry brought more tears to her eyes. She was pretty confident that he would be fine, but she needed him beside her; not in jail.

"I'll call you back once I find out more information, babe," Christian spoke to her.

"Baby, I love you," Keisha spoke.

"I love you, too," Christian hung up the phone.

He leaned against the wall and exhaled sharply.

"You going to be okay?" the officer asked.

"I'll be fine."

***

"What have you all discussed?" Andrew asked as he sipped his coffee.

"Nothing," Christian started. "They came and arrested me, Mirandized me, and put me in a holding cell by myself."

Andrew looked at Christian sternly.

"This one's going to be tough," he admitted. "But it's not impossible. For as long as I've known you, you've always been an upstanding person."

"Thanks, Drew," Christian spoke as he twiddled his thumbs.

"Did you have on your body-cam at the time of the incident?" Andrew asked as he wrote on the notepad he retrieved from his pocket.

"Yes," Christian spoke.

"Did it capture everything that occurred?"

"It should," Christian spoke. "I haven't seen it," he shook his head. "I guess I wasn't thinking about it at the time."

"That could be the key to this case," Andrew replied. "Once you have your initial court date, we're going to file a motion for us to retrieve bodycam footage from the night of the shooting."

Christian agreed with a nod.

"I will need to know all of the details; why you pursued him, what happened during the pursuit, what verbal commands did you pass on? I need to know everything so that I can help you."

"I have nothing to hide," Christian immediately replied. "It was a clean shot," he slightly raised his tone.

"Well we have a ways to go," Andrew replied. "We will take this one step at a time and get this resolved."

Christian shook Andrew's hand.

5

"All rise for the honorable, Judge Tracy Sinclair," the bailiff called.
Christian and Andrew rose to their feet, as well as the rest of the
congregation.
Keisha couldn't take her eyes off of Christian during the ordeal. Although
she couldn't bear to see him in these conditions, she knew she had to be
strong for him.

The judge entered the room from her chambers and walked behind her
desk.
"Fuck," Christian whispered under his breath.
Strike one.
Christian lowered his head slightly as she took her seat.
"Please be seated," she announced.
The members of the courtroom took their seats and she proceeded.

"Mr. Tate, you are charged with first-degree murder, two counts of
aggravated battery, and three counts of official misconduct in the shooting
death of 18-year-old Benjamin Smith on March 2nd, 2019," Tracy cleared
her throat. "And how do you plead?"
Andrew whispered to Christian before he spoke.
"Not guilty, Your Honor," Christian spoke.

"Where are we with bail?" she asked the prosecutor.

"Attorney Judy Holloway, with the prosecution," the prosecutor began. "Your Honor, the defendant is charged with first-degree murder, two counts of aggravated battery, and three counts of official misconduct. We feel he is a danger to society and is a flight risk."

"Your Honor, my client has been on the police force for eleven years, and not once has he had to fire his weapon. He's already released his weapons back to the force and does not have access to his pension as of now. All he's ever done was watch out for the city and the people in it," Andrew argued.

"Until now," Judy stated sternly to Andrew before looking at the judge. "Your Honor, Mr. Tate fired his weapon and killed a young man at point-blank range."

"The suspect was a risk to my client's life," Andrew fought. "May God rest his soul, but the second he drew his weapon, he knew that it wasn't going to end well. My client even tried to perform C.P.R. on the young man; all he does is assist the world, even when the world does nothing but tear him down."

Christian felt good knowing that his lawyer had his best interest at heart and wasn't afraid to fight.

"All it takes is one shot," Judy argued. "That's what makes a menace."

"If that's the case, lock up every single person who's ever fired a weapon and deny them bail," Andrew bit back.

"You're making this seem like this case is—."

"Black versus white?" Andrew finished her statement.

"Order in this courtroom," Tracy pounded her gavel.

The two lawyers stopped arguing and Tracy proceeded.

"This case will not be handled like a circus," she spoke. "A young man lost his life and an officer's life is at stake; this is a serious matter and with everything that's currently going on, I don't want for this to be made into a media frenzy."

She sifted through some papers.

"Bail is denied," she spoke.

Christian's heart sunk to his stomach as he heard these words: he could only imagine how Keisha was feeling.

"Your Honor," Andrew argued.

"The defendant will be taken into police custody and placed in a maximum-security prison pending trial."

Tracy hit her gavel and left the room.

"Don't even worry," Andrew spoke to Christian. "Just a minor setback but don't let this get to your head."

Christian turned around and Keisha quickly embraced him.

"Baby, I love you," she cried into his shirt.

"I'll be okay, babe," Christian kissed her forehead as officers approached him.

"Officers, can you give him a moment?" Andrew spoke to the officers as they approached.

Christian embraced Keisha.

"I don't want to let you go," she mentioned.

"It will be okay. I will call you once I get a chance," he kissed her forehead once more.

A tear fell from his eye and Keisha continued to sob into his shirt.

He patted her on the back and the officers patted him on the shoulders.

"Drew, I don't want to go into maximum security," he spoke as he was escorted away from Keisha. "If I want to be seen as a regular individual, I need to be among the general population. I'll be good," Christian finished before the police escorted him to the back.

"I'll talk to the judge and see what can be done."

The court officers escorted Christian from the courtroom and the tears continued to flow down Keisha's face.

Andrew shook his head and turned to face Keisha.

"He doesn't want to be in maximum security," he sighed.

"What?!" Keisha asked in shock.

"It seems like his mind is made up," Andrew replied as he held his briefcase. "I'm going to talk to him tomorrow before I go to the judge about it."

"Does he realize how much of a target he will be?" she asked rhetorically.

"He will be killed on sight," Keisha shook her head.

She opened her clutch handbag and pulled out a check.

She passed it to Andrew.

He declined the check.

"Keep it, Keisha," he announced. "Christian is a good friend and I couldn't take the money at a time like this. When we win, then you can pay me," he passed her the check and smiled.

Keisha embraced Andrew.

"Thank you," she spoke softly.

***

Christian's ride to the police station was silent; he was trying his hardest to process what was occurring.

The judge had just denied him bail, which means he would have to sit in prison until the trial, and there was no telling when that would be.

The van arrived in the prison yard and the guard unlocked the door.

Christian emerged from the vehicle in an orange jumpsuit with handcuffs on his hands.

He looked around and saw many inmates sitting in the yard playing cards, talking, and some were playing basketball.

Some of the prisoners looked at the van to see the newcomers.

"Christian Tate," the guard shook his head. "You've put a lot of people in here, man. Never did I expect to see you in here like this."

"Yeah, well Jimmy, I never expected to be here like this either," Christian spoke.

Jimmy held Christian's arm and walked him to the door of the building.

Jimmy held his badge to the scanner and the door unlocked. He opened the door and they walked inside.

"Chris, it's best if you keep your head down in here," Jimmy spoke. "There are a lot of criminals in here who would honestly do what they have to in order to kill a cop and once they find out you're on the inside, they're going to be all over it."

"I'll be fine," he spoke to Jimmy. "Thanks, Jim."

Jimmy slightly shook his head and continued to escort Christian to his maximum-security cell.

Jimmy closed the cell door and Christian took a seat on the bench. He couldn't stop his thoughts from racing.
"Day one," he stated aloud as he closed his eyes.
As quickly as he closed his eyes, he had to open them.

"Sergeant Christian Tate," an inmate spoke to him through the slot that separated the two cells.
Christian looked at the slot and saw the eyes of one of the inmates.
He walked closer to the hole and cracked his knuckles.
The inmate laughed.
"Nah, there's no need for that. I'm just letting you know that I know who you are.
"What do you want?" Christian asked.
"I don't want shit," he spoke gruffly. "But a lot of us here are hailing you as a hero," the inmate spoke. "Even though you put a lot of us in here, we're going to protect you."
"A hero?" Christian asked. "Why do you see me as a hero?"

The inmate chuckled lightly.
"Well, for one, you remember the Wallace case?"
"What about it?"
"There were some people protesting outside of a store and the police were called. You showed up to the scene with a lady cop and the store owner was acting crazy. You arrested her and afterward, you walked back up to this young man and gave him your card."
Christian knew who he was talking about.
"That's my son," the inmate laughed lightly. "And besides, after what you did to Benajmin Smith, that's one less racist bigot on the streets," he spoke. "We know it wasn't intentional, but we recognize that you're all about helping people, especially *our* people."
Christian was silent.

"Name's Raymond Farris, but everyone calls me Ray. Also known as The Alpha," the inmate continued. "I'll make sure you stay protected," he finished.

"What are you in for, Raymond?" Christian asked.

"Armed robbery," Raymond answered. "Shit, I didn't have any money and my daughter had to eat," he slightly shrugged his shoulders. "And you know as well as I do that once you check that box on your application that says you've been convicted, no one will hire your black ass," he chuckled.

Christian cleared his throat.

"How long are you in for?"

"Judge has given me 15 years," he added. "This isn't my first offense." Christian shook his head slightly.

"My daughter is with her mom," Raymond spoke. "Her mom was sick at the time; so I also had to get some money to help with those bills."

Sometimes, the law didn't make sense to Christian, although he wouldn't speak on it. While he didn't agree with Raymond stealing, he understood why he did it.

"Tell you what," Christian spoke. "You help me, and I'll help you. I'll speak to my lawyer about helping you get out of here. Get you back to your daughter and wife," he completed his sentence.

Raymond scratched his beard and continued.

"Don't even worry about it," he told Christian. "I did the crime so I have to face the repercussions of my actions. As long as my family is straight, I'm good."

"It's not fair to you though," Christian expressed his thoughts.

"Don't worry about it, Boss," Raymond projected. "While you're here, me and my boys will keep you safe. You have my word."

Christian nodded his head and Raymond closed the slot.

He walked over to the bed and laid down on it.

***

"Christian Tate, your lawyer is here," the guard spoke as he unlocked the gate to the cell.

Christian rose to his feet and the guard escorted him to a room where Andrew resided.

Christian sat and the guard closed the door to the room.

"What's going on?" Andrew asked.

"Nothing much. Just trying to get acclimated to this life. Who knows how long I will be in here," Christian replied unenthusiastically.

"Well we're not going to get anywhere if you're going to be negative about it," Andrew sat erect and Christian did the same. "How was your first night?"

"Hard, next question," Christian chuckled slightly.

Andrew chuckled.

"I met an inmate," Christian spoke. "He knew who I was right away."

"Wait, really?" Andrew shook his head.

"It wasn't even like that," Christian started. "His son was involved in the protest that happened right after the Wallace verdict, and I made sure his son was straight. He got booked for armed robbery; he was doing what he had to do to support his family," he popped his neck. "He told me that he and his crew were behind me and supported me."

"So, you're in here making friends?" Andrew asked with a slight laugh.

"He's a good guy," Christian defended. "He just got caught up in a bad situation," he paused. "I want for you to look up his case and see if you can help him out."

Andrew looked at Christian inquisitively.

"Why don't we focus on your case for now?" he suggested. "We need to get you out of here."

Christian interjected.

"I want you to look into his case," Christian reiterated.

Andrew sighed.

"I'll look into it. But I need you to keep your head in the game."

Christian nodded his head.

"Were you able to get the body cam footage?" he asked.

"I filed a motion for the judge to get the Miami P-D to release it," Andrew answered. "But I want to talk to you about wanting to switch to general population instead of maximum security."

"What about it?" Christian asked.

Andrew shook his head.
"It's a wild idea, Chris. You are a cop and you've put a lot of people in this prison."
"If I want to be seen as a regular, I shouldn't be in maximum security," Christian showed no fear.
"You could be killed on-sight if the judge places you in general population. You have to think about what you're saying," Andrew clarified.
Christian thought for a moment.
He knew that Andrew wouldn't change his stance; Christian understood that Andrew was concerned for his safety, but Christian felt that he would be fine.
Christian decided to compromise.
"I'll sleep in maximum security, but during the day, put me in general population," he negotiated.
"I don't know what judge would do that," Andrew mumbled, "but I'll talk to her."

"How's my wife?" Christian asked.
"She's hanging in there for you," he replied, "but I can tell it's hard. Seeing them take you away yesterday had her in tears."
Christian cleared his throat and shook his head.
"Make sure my baby is well," he spoke.
"She'll be fine. I'm sure she'll be up here to see you soon."
"Just let her know how much I love her and how I wish I was near her," Christian continued. "At least until she comes up here."
"I will," Andrew agreed.
Andrew looked at the clock on the wall.
"I'm going to get out of here and try to catch the judge. I'm going to get this request in as soon as possible so we keep the ball rolling."
"Thanks, Drew," Christian spoke. "Call me crazy, but I feel like I can learn a lot from these inmates and I feel like they can learn a lot from me," he shrugged his shoulders. "Besides, what have I got to lose?"

"You're a brave soul," Andrew put his hand on Christian's shoulder as he rose to his feet. "I'm also going to work on getting that body-cam footage. It's our key to beating this case."

"Drew," Christian spoke as the officers entered the room to escort him out. Andrew looked at Christian.

"Work quickly, okay?" Christian forced a smile.

Andrew tapped his chest and extended his arm to hold out his fist.

The officers escorted Christian from the room and Andrew left the facility.

6

"You're telling me that your client wants to be in general population?"
Tracy asked as she walked over to her bookshelf. "Does he realize that he's
a former Miami police officer?"
"I spoke to him, but he's adamant about this request. He's requesting to
spend his evenings in maximum security but to be amongst the general
population during the day."
Tracy looked at Andrew inquisitively.
"Does he have any special reasoning for requesting this?" she asked.
"He wants to earn respect from the inmates, and he feels the best way to do
that is to build a rapport with them."
Tracy shook her head lightly.
"He realizes that there are many souls there that wish to kill him, correct?"
Tracy slightly chuckled.
Andrew didn't mention what Raymond told Christian.
He shrugged his shoulders.

"This case is getting wilder by the minute," Tracy continued. "I already
have to sign these forms for the media explaining what I will allow and
won't allow in the courtroom, and now your client wishes to be moved into
the general population."
She looked at the clock on her wall.

"Let's walk and talk," she spoke to Andrew as she grabbed her phone and placed it in her pocket.

Andrew exited the office and she closed the door behind him. She locked the door before they walked away.

"I have a 3 o'clock case to get back to," she power walked.

"Your Honor, I know you're a busy woman," Andrew acknowledged. "So if we can get this resolved as quickly as possible, I can let you get back to your duties," Andrew walked alongside her.

"Mr. Brownstone," she started, "have you spoken to the prosecution about this motion?"

"I haven't, Your Honor, but I don't see how this matter concerns the prosecution when my client is already being remanded until trial and his bail was denied," Andrew shook his head.

"Mr. Brownstone, even if I were to sign this paper for you, it would get back to the prosecution, and if the D.A. disagrees..."

"I thought you were in charge," Andrew challenged her with a smirk.

Tracy stopped walking and looked at Andrew.

"You're not going to let this go with a 'no', are you?" she asked.

Andrew reached in his briefcase and pulled out a manilla folder.

He reached into the folder and pulled out a piece of paper.

"I just need for you to sign right here," Andrew spoke with a smile.

Tracy smirked and shook her head.

She took a pen from her pocket and signed the paperwork.

"Is there anything else, Mr. Brownstone?" she asked as he put the form in the folder.

"There is one more thing," he spoke. "My client and I would like to file a motion to retrieve the bodycam footage on the night of the shooting."

"I'm surprised the police department hasn't given that to you," Tracy spoke. "I'll get that motion to you. Bring me the paperwork for it and I'll sign it."

"Funny you said that," Andrew pulled out another piece of paper from the folder. "Just need a signature on the line."

Tracy skimmed over the paper.
"Are you always this efficient?" she asked Andrew.
"Contrary to what you may believe, *we* enjoy getting the job done," he hinted at the stereotype of African Americans being lazy. "Thank you for your time and signatures, Your Honor," he finished.
Tracy couldn't say much after his comment.
Andrew parted ways from Tracy and returned the folder to his briefcase.
He dialed Keisha's number on the phone.

"Hello?" she answered.
"I got the judge to sign the motion for the bodycam," he spoke excitedly.
"We're going to have Christian home soon," he replied.
"I just got off the phone with him," Keisha spoke. "He's adamant about being moved into general population, huh?" she asked.
"I can't change his mind," Andrew spoke. "I got the judge to sign that motion as well. But," he continued, "he wants to spend his nights in solitary confinement; the days will be amongst the inmates. Apparently, one of the inmates spoke to him yesterday and the inmate told Christian that he supported him and felt that the shooting was justified. He told Christian that he would look out for him," Andrew finished as he approached his car.

"He needs to worry about his own safety before worrying about getting in good with the other inmates," Keisha shook her head.
"I'm on my way back there now to present this to the officers. One, so that I can get the bodycam footage, and two so that his wish to be amongst G.P. is fulfilled."
"Well, let me let you get back to it," she expressed.
"Okay, Keish. Keep your head up," he spoke.
Andrew hung up the phone and walked to his vehicle.
He was swarmed by the paparazzi crew.
"Mr. Brownstone, we have word that your client may be looking to appeal the judge's decision to deny bail," a reporter shouted.

Andrew ignored the comment.

"Mr. Brownstone, any word of how Mr. Tate is holding up in jail?" another reporter asked.

"Mr. Tate is doing just fine," Andrew spoke.

"Mr. Brownstone, a lot of people are calling this the case of the year," another woman shouted. "Primarily because of the Wallace case that just ended, in which you had a White officer shoot and kill a Black teenager. Now, you have the Florida v. Tate case, which features a Black cop shooting and killing a White teenager. Do you think that race was a factor in Christian Tate's decision to pursue and kill Benjamin Smith?" she finished.

Andrew processed what she said before replying.

"Who are you with?" he asked.

"Channel 8 news," she replied.

"That explains it," he scoffed. "My client did not pursue the subject because of his skin tone, nor did the Wallace verdict have anything to do with his decision. The truth is that as he apprehended the subject, Mr. Smith pulled out a firearm and aimed it at my client. Now, the media, which is all of you," Andrew spoke, "you all are going to make this a case about race. Which, you know, I understand; it's your job to keep the media entertaining, but before you report information, please make sure you have your facts straight."

Andrew cleared his throat.

"Now, if you all will excuse me, I have a job to do as well."

Andrew opened his car door and got inside.

"Mr. Brownstone!" reporters continued to shout.

Andrew revved his engine and made the exhaust emit a popping noise.

As the reporters cleared the way, Andrew drove away.

***

"Good news," Andrew sat across from Christian. "I got the judge to sign and approve both of our requests."

"Okay," Christian expressed. "So, where's the footage?"

"It's on this flash drive," Andrew spoke as he pulled out the device.

Andrew also pulled his laptop from his briefcase.

"I haven't seen it yet, so this will be my first time as well."

The two of them watched the video together.

Watching the video quickly took Christian back to the day.

"*Miami P-D, freeze!*" he shouted over the video.

Christian shook his head as he saw Benjamin Smith running.

"*If you don't stop, you will be tased,*" Christian recalled all of his thoughts at the time.

"See, right there is where I gave the verbal warning of releasing a non-lethal tasing," he spoke to Andrew.

Andrew nodded his head in agreement and continued to watch as Benjamin arrived at the gate.

The video was jumpy and had moments where it was hard to focus on what was going on, but that was to be expected since it was bodycam footage.

Christian watched as Benjamin fell off of the fence.

Christian shook his head as he watched the camera move towards Benjamin's body.

"Fuck you, man," Benjamin shouted as he tried to stand.

Christian saw his hand extend and push Benjamin back on the ground. He heard the chain links on the handcuffs and saw them come into view.

Out of his peripheral vision, he saw Andrew shake his head.

The camera showed Benjamin leap to his feet and reach around to his back pocket.

"*Drop your weapon,*" Christian spoke as Benjamin jumped to his feet.

He saw Benjamin put the weapon in his waistband and begin running.

Andrew heard Christian breathing heavily as the screen was shaky from the running.

The screen went black and Andrew heard a fall.

"What the hell?" Andrew asked.

"*Stay on your stomach and extend your arms, let me see your hands! Drop your weapon,*" he heard Christian shout over the recording.

Suddenly, a gunshot was heard which made Andrew jump a little.

"What just happened?" Christian asked. "Why did the screen go black?"

"I have to ask you the same question," Andrew replied.

"*Shots fired! I need an ambulance—*" Andrew stopped the recording.

"I need to know why the video feed ended," Christian shook his head. "My camera was on the entire time."

"I can see it was recording because the audio is there," Andrew spoke.

Christian was confused.

Andrew shook his head.

"Are you sure this is the original recording?" Christian asked.

"It's the one that was given to me by the station," Andrew replied.

"Something's not right," Christian kept his hands visible on the table.

Andrew rewound the video to where it went black.

"*Drop your weapon,*" Christian shouted after the camera went black.

"The most crucial part of the video isn't here," Andrew shook his head.

"But we can work with the audio, correct?" Christian asked.

"We can try, but it's going to be a long shot," Andrew admitted. "But don't let this discourage you. We are going to win this case," he spoke, sounding confident.

Christian decided it would be best to change the subject to keep a positive outlook.

"So, how is this going to work? Am I going to be transferred on a daily and nightly basis?"

"That's exactly what's going to happen," Andrew answered. "So don't get too comfortable amongst the people," he chuckled.

"I'm going to make sure they love me," Christian replied.

Andrew chuckled.

"Well, while you're doing that, I'm going to work on figuring this case out. Don't even worry about it."

***

"Christian Tate," an inmate called as he approached the table that Christian resided.

Christian looked over his shoulder and saw the man approaching him.

Christian rose to his feet in case he would have to defend himself.

"We got this, Boss," Raymond spoke to Christian as he put a hand on his shoulder.

"Tell your goons to stand down," the man chuckled. "It's not necessary for me… even if you did put me in here," he continued.

"What's up?" Christian spoke.

"The word around camp is that you're in here for murder."

"I'd use that term loosely," Christian spoke to the man. "The young man pulled out a gun on me and I defended myself," he explained.

"Yeah, yeah. It was either your life or his, right?" the inmate questioned.

Christian got a better look at the inmate before speaking.

"Derrick Gaines," he spoke as he recalled who he was.

"Ding ding ding," the inmate chuckled. "I knew you'd remember me."

"Murder trial back in 2016. You were in an altercation with an individual; he was on the ground and you drew your firearm and fired a fatal shot into his head. Your defense was— "

"Self defense," Derrick finished his sentence with a laugh. "Not much fun when the rabbit has the gun, huh?"

Christian shook his head.

"Now, I should be all over you for taking away 25 years of my life," he started.

Christian already knew this would be the case with many inmates in the jail: he knew they would approach him with threats.

"But I'm not going to do that," Derrick continued. "Nah, karma is a bitch and she's coming at you fast." He looked at Raymond and then back at Christian. "The crazy part is, is that I looked all of you in the face and told you that even though he was on the ground, I felt threatened, and you let your fuckin' D.A. sit there and tell me that there was no way someone on the ground could be seen as a threat."

Christian felt bad by hearing this. He remembered the case vividly, and everything Derrick was saying was true.

"But you know what, I commend you. Although you let them put me in here, you have always represented for your people," Derrick cleared his throat. "I believe that cracka' pulled a gun out on you and tried to kill you; sounds like something they would do."

Christian didn't show signs of agreement with Derrick's racist argument, even if he did agree with what he was saying.

"Always trying to keep the Black man down," Derrick added. "This is why if you cooperate and things go as they should, you have the support of my crew while you're in here."

Christian looked Derrick in the eyes but remained silent.

"Not going to lie to you; you're probably one of the most respected officers that have been put in the pin," Derrick finished. "Keep your head."

Derrick extended his hand for a shake and Christian accepted.

Derrick and his posse walked off and Christian returned to his seat.

"You knew this was going to be the case, huh?" Raymond asked.

"You have no idea," Christian responded. "But hey, I got my lawyer looking into your case," he spoke to Raymond.

"Word?" Raymond asked. "What's his name?"

"His name is Andrew Brownstone," Christian replied.

"Is he…?" Raymond tapped his skin.

"Yeah, he's one of us," Christian replied as he knew what Raymond was referring to. "Do you have a lawyer?" he asked Raymond.

"Well, you know that once the case is over, they pretty much move on," Raymond shrugged his shoulders. "Especially these public defenders when you can't necessarily afford a lawyer."

"It's this system," Christian popped his neck. "But the next time he's up here, I'm going to ask him to speak to you."

"I'd appreciate that," Raymond confessed. "Good lookin'."

"No doubt," Christian spoke.

Raymond rose to his feet as the prison guard entered the room of inmates.

"How you girls doing?" the guard humiliated them.

Christian also stood.

"You girlies wanna see sunlight?" he asked in a mocking tone.

None of the inmates replied.

"We're gonna let the house niggers out first," he ridiculed, referencing the inmates with a lighter complexion.

"Deputy Tanner!" Christian spoke aloud.

The prison guard scanned the room to see who spoke aloud.

"Which one of you sissies spoke out of turn?"

"I did," Christian spoke as he stepped forward. "Sergeant- I mean, Christian Tate," he finished.

"Well, if it isn't the cop," Deputy Tanner spoke loudly.

Christian didn't back down.

"Why don't you get your black ass back in line?"

"Who made you this way?" Christian immediately rebutted.

"Are you questioning my authority?" the guard asked.

"You're damn right, I am," Christian answered.

Deputy Tanner walked up to Christian and was nose-to-nose with him.

"Last time I checked, you had your badge stripped away. So you best fall back in line, nigger," Deputy Tanner snarled.

Christian didn't back down.

"It's funny to me," he started.

"What the fuck's funny?" Deputy Tanner asked.

"You realize that you're one of us," Christian immediately replied. "With or without that badge, the system sees you as just another Black man," Christian didn't use racial slurs.

The inmates watched as Christian went back-and-forth with the deputy.

"What makes you think we're on the same playing field?" Deputy Tanner asked.

"Well, Charles," Christian used the deputy's first name. "For starters, I was in a position higher than you," he smirked. "And as soon as things got out of hand, they labeled me as an angry, out-of-control, Black man. Man, look at the media. They're having a field day bashing my name, when, not to brag, I was one of the best things that happened to the force."

"You really think we're alike, huh?" Charles scoffed. "Nigger, I wouldn't be in your shoes nor would I want to be in your shoes, even if Donald Trump were to pay me."

"And you," Christian continued, "you're the exact definition of being lost and hating one's self. You don't know who you really are. Your self-hatred is disgusting, and I recommend you get some help for that," Christian finished. "At the end of the day, the system will always see you as just another Black man. You determine whether you use that to your advantage or disadvantage," he slightly shrugged his shoulders.

Charles didn't like that he was being challenged, especially by a former police officer.

Charles reached on his side for his baton but didn't feel it.

"You feeling for something?" Christian spoke as he showed Charles the baton. "If you were really doing your job, you would know to never get close enough to an inmate or get so involved where they could disarm you or gain control of your weapons."

Christian knew he was taking a huge risk in showing Charles that he took the baton, but he was in too deep. He couldn't back down.

"In this case, I took control of the biggest weapon there is: your mind," Christian added. "When I took control of that, I was able to control everything around you; including your baton. You were distracted: terrible for a deputy."

Charles was humiliated and he didn't like the feeling.

He discreetly felt on his other side and unstrapped the pocket. He pulled out the taser and tased Christian.

The alarm in the prison sounded and Charles stood over Christian.

Christian fell to his knees and the inmates started shouting.

Christian let out a silent cry.

"Look at you now, Nigger. Who's on whose level now?" he asked.

Charles picked up the baton as Christian rose to his feet.

Charles held the baton and ran into Christian, pushing him back against the wall. He held the baton against Christian's neck to pin him.

Christian gasped for air and used his strength the separate the baton from his neck.

"Just like an Uncle Tom," Christian shouted.

Raymond intervened and grabbed Charles and pulled him off of Christian. He flung Charles down to the ground.

"You okay?" Raymond quickly asked as he got back on defense in case Charles was to attempt to fire back.

"I'm good," Christian spoke.

Charles rose to his feet and spoke into his shoulder.

Charles popped his neck.

"We have a situation here in cell block 'D'," he finished.

Charles reached for Raymond and Christian extended his arms to separate the two.

"Assaulting an officer; you're going down," Charles spoke as he breathed heavily.

"Calm it down," Christian tried to de-escalate the situation.

More officers ran into the room with guns aimed.

"Get down!" they shouted.

All of the inmates laid on the floor, including Christian and Raymond. The room seemed to silence in an instant.

Charles wiped his nose as he glared at Christian.

"Deputy Thomas," an officer approached. "Are these the culprits?" he asked as he looked at Christian and Raymond.

Charles wiped his nose as he thought about everything Christian said to him.

"Yeah, that's them," he spoke gruffly. "Take them to solitary confinement. A week," he finished.

"Let's go," the officer spoke to the two with his weapon aimed.

Christian and Raymond both rose to their feet and two other officers approached.

They placed them both in handcuffs and escorted them from the room. The inmates cheered from the floor as Christian and Raymond were escorted out.

7

Christian entered the courtroom wearing a suit and spotted Andrew sitting.
He saw Keisha dressed in a black dress.
She blew him a kiss as he walked behind the desk.
Christian sat down next to Andrew.
"How's everything been since that day?" he whispered.
"Just taking this shit day-by-day," Christian whispered back. "I have to get
back home to my baby."
"We got this," Andrew spoke confidently.
"All rise for the honorable, Judge Tracy Sinclair," the bailiff announced.
Everyone rose to their feet.
Once the judge entered the room and sat, everyone else sat.
"Today we will begin jury selection," she announced. "But before we do
that, I have been made aware of an incident that occurred in the jailhouse
on June 5th at approximately 12 pm," she shuffled the papers. "Mr. Tate,
Deputy Charles Thomas has told the court that you incited a riot, and as a
result, you and another inmate were placed in solitary confinement for a
week."
Tracy wanted to shake her head but didn't.
"What do you have to say about this?" she asked him.

Christian whispered to Andrew.

"Go on," Andrew spoke softly.

"Your Honor, I didn't incite a riot," Christian spoke. "Deputy Thomas incited the riot himself by abusing his power. We had an exchange of words, and he quickly became aggressive and physical; he tased me and pinned me against the wall with his baton," he defended.

"This behavior is unacceptable," Tracy spoke. "Between both you and the deputy," she placed the folder down. "I will put this charge on hold until I'm able to review jailhouse tapes to confirm either yours or the deputy's stories. But you should know better than to mouth off with a prison guard," she sternly addressed Christian.

Christian nodded his head and Tracy continued.

"Have the questionnaires been reviewed by both parties?" she asked the lawyers.

"Yes, Your Honor," Andrew spoke.

"Yes, Your Honor," Judy spoke. "The prosecution is ready for the selection process."

"Let's get this started," Tracy spoke.

Christian watched as the lawyers began to thoroughly question each potential juror.

Although several different questions were asked to each juror, he noticed a few questions that were similar from both lawyers: 'how did you feel about the Wallace verdict?' and 'have you or a family member or friend been a victim of police brutality; particularly of an officer of a different race?' Although they phrased it differently amongst the jurors, the questions continued to arise.

Hours passed as Christian watched the lawyers go back and forth with the jurors.

"That's all of the jurors," Tracy spoke.

The two lawyers approached the judge's desk.

"Begin," Tracy spoke as she held her pen to her notepad.

The two lawyers began to list which jurors they were choosing to eliminate.

Christian looked back at Keisha and watched as tears flowed from her eyes.

"I love you," he mouthed out.

She crossed her heart with her finger.

"I love you, too," she mouthed out.

Moments later, Christian saw Andrew returning to the desk. Judy also returned to hers.

"We will reconvene on Monday," Tracy spoke. "The jurors have been selected and we will begin with opening arguments."

Tracy hit her gavel.

"All rise!" the bailiff spoke.

Everyone rose to their feet and Tracy exited the room.

"Sit tight for now," Andrew spoke to Christian. "We've been prepping for months, and now it's showtime," he adjusted Christian's collar.

"Thanks for everything, Drew," Christian spoke as the court officer walked over and took his arm.

Christian put his hands in front of him and the officer secured the cuffs.

"Can I say a few words to my wife?" Christian spoke.

"Go on," the officer spoke.

Christian walked towards the gate and Keisha walked up to him.

"How are you doing, babe?" he asked.

"Taking it day-by-day, you know?" she forced a chuckle as a tear rolled down her cheek.

"I'm sorry for putting you through this," he spoke. "It will all be over soon."

Keisha leaned over and hugged him. She gave him a kiss on the lips and patted his chest.

"I'll come visit you this evening," she spoke.

"Okay, babe," Christian spoke softly.

"Come on," the officer spoke gently as he tugged at Christian's arm.

"I love you," Christian added.

"I love you, too," Keisha replied.

The court officer walked Christian to the back and handed him to another police officer.

The officer walked Christian to the police van and exchanged no words. He opened the back and Christian climbed inside.

"Can y'all be sure to turn on the A.C.?" Christian chuckled. "This Florida sun is no joke."

The officer didn't reply. He closed the doors.

Christian looked around the van; he knew he would be the only one riding in it, considering the nature of the case.

His thoughts roamed as the van door opened.

A lady officer sat in the back before closing the door behind her. The van began to move and Christian put his head on the wall of the van.

"Christian Tate," she spoke.

"Yes," he replied with his eyes closed.

"How did it go?" she asked him.

"It's a lot," he never opened his eyes.

Although the sun was shining through the windows of the van, Christian could still feel a cold chill running down his body.

"The jury has been selected; I haven't seen exactly who was kept and dismissed, but I'll find out soon. Opening statements are Monday," Christian twiddled his thumbs.

The officer put her hand on his shoulder.

"It'll be okay," she whispered. "You have mine and many other officers' support."

Christian was silent.

He was still trying to wrap his mind around what was occurring.

He was a prisoner for doing his job. He couldn't help but relate it to the Wallace case, where the officer was found not guilty *and* he got to keep his job.

But Christian knew his career was over and tainted. Even if he was found not guilty, he wouldn't be able to land a job with this over his head. He would have to start fresh with a new career.

'Maybe a mall would hire me as a security guard,' he joked to himself as he felt the van drive over small bumps.

He knew from this that they were arriving at the prison's lot.

The van came to a stop and Christian heard the door unlock.

He lifted his head and sat up.

The officer jumped down from the van and Christian rose to his feet.

He walked to the exit and two officers helped him down from the platform. Christian used his hands to block the sun.

"We're going to take you into general population for dinner," the officer spoke. "And then you'll be escorted back to your cell around 9:30."

"Sounds good," Christian stated.

The officers walked him into the prison and removed his handcuffs. Christian was escorted to the cellblock where the inmates resided. They were all talking amongst each other, some were watching the small television in the corner, and some were reading and responding to letters.

Christian walked over to Raymond and stood tall.

"How'd it go?" Raymond asked as he did pushups.

Christian crouched down.

"Jury selection," he responded. "Nothing to it. We start trial on Monday."

"It's been about six months, right?" Raymond asked as he pushed faster.

"Much too long," Christian shrugged his shoulders. "What about you? What's going on with everything?"

"Just taking life one day at a time," Raymond spoke in between sets. He rose to his feet and stretched his muscles.

"You know they gave a nigga years."

"What about Andrew?" Christian asked. "He hasn't spoken to you?"

"I haven't heard much from him. I've accepted my fate, Christian," Raymond spoke. "My focus is to be sure that you get the justice you deserve."

"You sound just like him," Christian chuckled. "You sure you haven't spoken to him?"

Raymond spoke with a serious tone.

"Christian, you are a cop. A cop with a bright future who did something that took tremendous courage. This isn't the end for you."

"And it's not the end for you either. I'm going to fight for you to beat this shit. And once we're free, you can come through for a lil' one-on-one in ball," Christian spoke.

Raymond clapped hands with Christian.

"Let's get to work, then," he replied.

Christian nodded his head and the buzzer rang to let the inmates know that it was dinner time.

"I'm going to talk to Andrew tomorrow," Christian spoke as he and Raymond walked to the dinner line.

"Okay, cool," Raymond uttered.

Raymond stood behind Christian as they each walked in the line to get their dinner trays.

Christian placed his hand on the metal bar and felt how cold it was to touch.

"You good?" Raymond asked as he saw Christian paused.

Christian couldn't help but think about Keisha and how much he missed her; how greatly this case must have been affecting her.

"Yo, you good?" Raymond asked again.

"My bad," Christian replied as he stepped forward. "It's just that this whole thing is in my head now," he shook his head. "Just thinking about my wife and how it must be affecting her."

"When was the last time you spoke to her?" Raymond asked as the two stepped away from the line with their food.

"Earlier today," Christian spoke. "But I gotta get out of here," his voice quivered. "I know she's not holding up well, regardless of what she said."

Raymond shook his head and put a hand on Christian's shoulder.

"You're going to get through this," he replied. "You just have to keep your head held high."

"This shit is tough," Christian admitted.

He and Raymond walked over to an empty table and sat.

"So," Raymond took a bite of the sandwich, "tell me how this is supposed to go down," he started.

"In terms of your trial?" Christian asked.

"The whole process," Raymond spoke. "You know, a nigga like me has literally lost all hope. Who would have thought I would get it back from a cop?" he chuckled.

"Inspiration came come from the weirdest places," Christian replied. "You're giving me the inspiration to keep pushing. We don't deserve to be in this hellhole," he lowered his tone to a whisper.

"Same shit I've been saying," Raymond laughed.

"Keep it down," Christian chuckled. "But, I'm going to tell you now; these next steps are going to go by fast."

"I'm ready for it," Raymond replied.

"Dre is going to try your case, but you have to be ready to give your best effort," Christian spoke. "You have to be on your best behavior in here and ready to give him what he needs to proceed. No smart remarks or comments; especially because he's going to move quickly and doesn't need anything stopping the process."

"Hey man," Raymond spoke. "I am ready and willing to get this started and get this out of the way," he took a sip of his water. "I'll have to start life over, but I can do it."

"Let's do it then," Christian spoke.

The two of them ate their food and conversed as time passed by.
A guard entered the hall and called out.
"Christian Tate, front and center."

Christian walked to the front and approached Charles.
"You have a visitor," he spoke with his head high.
"That's that cop bullshit," an inmate yelled. "It's beyond visiting hours."
Christian and Charles ignored the inmate and Charles walked Christian out of the lobby.
Christian sat at the table and awaited his visitor.
A smile formed across his face as he saw Keisha. This was the *only* person he'd wanted to see.
"Hey baby," Keisha spoke softly as she sat down across from Christian.
"You made it," he smiled. "I don't think you understand how happy I am to see you."
"I told you I was coming by," she replied. "How are things in there?"
Christian looked over his shoulder and saw Charles staring in his direction.

"Well, things would be better if this Uncle Tom wasn't breathing down my neck with every step I took," Christian shook his head.

"I heard that," Charles projected.

"See what I mean?" Christian whispered to his wife. "You were supposed to," he replied to Charles.

"Baby, things will get better," she promised Christian as she took his hand in hers.

"No touching," Charles spoke aloud.

Christian ignored him and continued to hold his wife's hand.

"How are things out there, Mama?" Christian asked Keisha.

"You know the media is having a field day with your case," she shrugged her shoulders. "They're making you out to be the bad guy. But you know that you have me and your family behind you," Keisha assured him.

"To hell with the media," Christian rebutted. "You and I both know where my heart is and intentions are. You know they're going to do everything they can to bring and to keep a black man down."

Keisha nodded her head in agreement.

"I know, babe," she responded. "But you just focus on beating this case. For me and your little one."

Christian raised his eyebrows.

"So, it's confirmed, babe?"

Keisha confirmed with a smile and nod.

"The baby and I are both relying on you to get through this," she confided as she rubbed her stomach.

"What has the doctor said?" Christian asked.

"She's healthy," Keisha replied. "But she's going to need her father."

His heart was full of joy, but he was worried about what his fate would be.

"I wish shit was different. I'm in jail for doing what I was taught to do... and now I don't know how things are going to be for my child."

"Don't talk like that," Keisha spoke sternly. "I need for you to be strong in here, just like I am out there."

She touched his chin and slightly lifted it.

"Look at me," she continued.

Christian looked at his wife.

"You knew when you took this job that the system wasn't meant to benefit *us* in any way, but you were determined to make a difference. And you've done that, and I am so proud of you, Christian. Keep your head up, baby. This will be over soon," she assured him.

Charles walked over; Christian saw him through his peripheral vision.

"Visitation is over, Tate," he spoke gruffly.

Keisha patted her hands on top of Christian's.

"I'll be back tomorrow, babe," she assured him.

"Okay, babe," Christian responded.

"And keep your head," she slowly rose to her feet.

She walked around and kissed him on the cheek.

"I love you," Christian spoke.

"I love you, too," Keisha replied.

Keisha walked towards the exit and Christian rose to his feet.

"You ready to go back with the other girls?" Charles mimicked.

Christian didn't give him the energy. He was too excited about having seen Keisha and hearing good news about his unborn child to entertain Charles' energy.

But Christian was also fearful for his wife and their child's life.

Charles escorted Christian back down to the hall with the other inmates; many of them gave Charles dirty looks.

Christian walked into the dining area and scanned the room.

He saw Raymond and walked over to him.

"Had fun with Charles?" Raymond joked with Christian.

"Funny guy," Christian replied. "What'd I miss?"

"Same old thing," Raymond spoke. "The only difference is that since Charles was gone with you, there was no one here to belittle us," he laughed. "What about you?"

"That was my wife," Christian smiled.

"You always light up when you're talking about her," Raymond spoke. "That's real love right there."

"Yeah, and I'm smiling even harder because of the news I just got," he was smiling from ear to ear.

"Damn, nigga. Spit it out. Whatever it is has got you brighter than these flashlights these officers carry," Raymond smirked.

"She's pregnant," Christian spoke, "and the baby is growing healthily. A little girl," Christian finished.

"Congratulations man," Raymond spoke after a few seconds of silence. He patted Christian on the shoulder.

"I don't know man," Christian started. "I'm excited, but I'm also worried for my wife and child. Let's be real, I'm in jail," he shook his head. "A Black man in jail for shooting a White kid. I can hear the death threats towards my wife and child now."

Raymond was speechless.

"And what makes it worse is that I'm in here. I'm not there to protect them if shit hits the fan."

"Man, we're going to get you out of here so don't even worry about that," Raymond assured him. "Your case starts Monday so now you're in the home stretch."

Christian scratched his chin.

"I'm not sure," he stated. "Honestly, one part of crucial evidence is fucked up. It can honestly go either way," Christian sounded slightly discouraged.

"We're going to make it work out," Raymond spoke. "Gotta keep the faith."

"Kind of hard to do in times like these," Christian confided.

"I know," Raymond spoke.

Moments later, Charles entered the hall with other officers; none were armed.

"Alright, ladies," he projected. "It's lights out. Everyone needs to report to their cells."

Christian and Raymond rose to their feet and made eye contact with Charles.

Charles smirked at the two and continued.

"Officers, please keep these inmates in line. I'm going to escort these two to their cells."

Charles stepped forward; Christian and Raymond never took their eyes off of him.

"If it isn't my favorite ladies," Charles chuckled in a whisper to the two. Christian nor Raymond showed any emotion.

"Let's go," he spoke.

Christian looked at Raymond and nodded. Charles felt offended as Raymond stepped forward.

"This black nigger doesn't tell you when to step," he asserted as they entered the corridor. "I do. I'm the king around here."

Raymond rolled his eyes. Christian looked at him as if to say 'just keep walking'.

"When I'm talking to you, you speak, Nigger," he asserted again.

"You still don't get it, do you?" Christian spoke.

"Are you speaking out of turn?" Charles asked Christian as the three continued to walk.

"The system is still viewing you as just another Black man; with or without that badge. Have you not learned anything from me being in here?" Christian asked.

"Nigger, we didn't come here in the same boat."

"I hate to tell you, but we are exactly alike. I've said it before and I'll say it again," Christian continued walking. "You're still a nigga."

"That's nigga, with an 'a'," Raymond chuckled.

Charles felt insulted by their comments. He thought of striking Raymond and Christian but remembered the previous encounter.

"Keep it moving," he firmly stated.

Christian and Raymond smirked at each other as they approached their cells.

Raymond entered his cell first, and Christian walked into his next.

Charles walked away.

"How did I get lucky enough to get a cell right beside you?" Christian joked.

"We both need that maximum security," Raymond laughed. "And plus, it's not bad that they put us beside each other," they spoke through the hole in the wall that separated the two cells.

"You're right," Christian spoke. "Check it out," he continued. "I'm going to speak with Drew tomorrow and have him speak with you. Now is the time to move."

"Your plan, my command," Raymond answered.

8

Christian entered the courtroom alongside two officers and they escorted him to the desk that Andrew stood. He stood next to his lawyer.
Christian spotted Keisha sitting in the front row behind Andrew. He blew her a kiss and she raised her hand as if she were catching it.
"So, I've been looking through the files," Andrew spoke in a whisper.
"Please tell me you've got some good news for me," Christian responded.
Andrew scoffed.
"I wish. I'm still investigating the video, but I haven't had any bit of luck. And it's messed up because the audio is there, but the video isn't. The P-D swears up and down that's all they have."
"Because that's the code," Christian spoke as he remembered the things that would be discussed in the office. "We protect our own. And right now, I'm not one of them."
"So, no protection," Andrew responded with a slight headshake.

"All rise," the bailiff announced.
Everyone in the courtroom rose to their feet.
"The honorable, Judge Tracy Sinclair presiding," the bailiff continued.
Tracy entered the courtroom from her chambers and sat behind her desk.
"You may be seated. Everyone needs to ensure that cellphones and other electronic devices are powered off," he instructed.

Christian looked around at the news cameras around the courtroom.

"Good morning, ladies and gentlemen," Tracy spoke. "Last time we saw each other, we finished selecting the jury. Today we will begin the case of *Florida v. Tate*. We are going to start with opening arguments from both sides."
Judy rose to her feet and walked from behind her desk.

Back at the prison, Raymond sat amongst the other inmates.
"Yo, pass me that remote," he spoke aloud.
As he received the remote, he turned on the television to Christian's court case.

"Good morning, everyone," Judy started. "Your Honor; ladies and gentlemen of the jury; Andrew; Christian; Christian's wife, Keisha; family and friends of Benjamin Smith. How is everyone doing today?" she rhetorically asked.
Christian didn't take his eyes off of her.
"There are limited situations in which sworn officer of the law; one who took an oath to serve and protect, may kill a citizen. On the evening of March 2nd, 2019, the defendant shot and killed 18-year-old Benjamin Smith. He shot Mr. Smith once in the chest after assaulting him and sending an electrical current through his body, also known as tasing him."
Christian glared at Judy as she spoke.

The part that was mindboggling to Christian was that she did plenty of work with him, so she knew that he was a good cop. But, at the same time, he realized she was a prosecutor with a job to do.
Christian glanced behind him and saw Theresa wiping tears from her eyes.

"When Mr. Tate shot Benjamin Smith, Benjamin was on the ground. Defenseless," she paced the floor in front of the jury. "On his stomach with arms stretched out. Stunned. Shooting him wasn't necessary and was an abuse of power."

Christian felt the sweat beading up on his forehead.

"It was late at night and it was raining; Benjamin was looking forward to his upcoming lockout that was held by the ROTC program at his school," Judy continued. "Christian Tate weighs about 220 pounds, whereas Benjamin weighs 165, fully drenched and clothed; yet Mr. Tate argues that he feared for his life." Judy inhaled and continued. "I will be walking you all through the dashcam video as we discuss this. All of this began with a 911call of a 'suspicious character' near 44th and Michigan," she walked to the smartboard where the streets were displayed. She picked up the marker and circled the intersection. Dispatch was unable to give a visual description of the suspect. Since Mr. Tate was in the vicinity, he took it upon himself to go check it out," Judy walked away from the board and back to the majority-white jury.

Christian could see the concerned looks on their faces and desperately wanted to defend his reason for going but didn't want to give the jury reason to believe the stereotype.

"Upon arrival, Mr. Tate saw Benjamin crouched between two bushes," she squatted down to demonstrate the position Benjamin was in. "Just like this," she clarified. "When Mr. Tate got out of his vehicle and spoke to Benjamin, fear filled his young body. Benjamin ran. Should he have run? No," she answered her own question, "but imagine being outside, late in the evening, and you have a large male speaking to you and approaching you," she referenced Christian's build. "Sure, you see the siren lights, but with everything going on, you couldn't be too sure that it was a real officer; so, out of fear, you run."

Christian nudged Andrew gently.

Andrew put his hand on Christian's shoulder.

"Benjamin, as you can see here," Judy followed the video, "reaches the gate and begins to climb in an attempt to get away from the defendant, and the defendant sends 1200 volts of electricity through Benjamin's body. As he returns to the Earth, you see the defendant linger over his body," Judy continued.

Christian watched the jury's reactions as they saw Benjamin pull out the firearm, yet return it to his waistband and start running.

"Ladies and gentlemen, I warn you; this is where things go dark; literally and figuratively," Judy continued to pace the floor while holding the remote. "You see and hear the defendant running, but that will change in 3, 2, 1," the screen went black but the audio could be heard. "While you can not see anything," she added, "you can hear someone fall and the defendant shout, 'stay on your stomach' and 'drop your weapon', before the deadly shot was fired. But," she raised her eyebrow, "the last we saw, Benjamin returned his weapon to his waist. You're telling me he pulled it out while running?" she asked rhetorically.

"I know you better have a hell of an opening argument," Christian whispered to Andrew.

"Shh," he shushed Christian.

"There's a reason the video went dark," Judy spoke as she pressed pause on the remote. "I trust that you see that reason, but if you need any reassurance, we will prove it to you."

Judy looked at Christian before walking to her seat.

Andrew rose to his feet and approached the jury.

"On the evening of March 2nd, 2019, Christian Tate was on duty, covering for one of his fellow officers," Andrew spoke. "11 years on the force; five years without having to fire his weapon. One thing happens when he has to use his power, boom; they strip all of his rights and throw him into the cell," Andrew knew the jury had a majority of Caucasian individuals; mostly females, so he had to find a way to tug at their emotions.

"My client has numerous awards, badges, and has been commended numerous times by his ranking officers, leaders, and even the prosecutor," he pointed to Judy, "but none of that means anything, right?" he chuckled as he stepped towards the jury.

"Now, I'm going to walk you all through what happened; similar to what Ms. Holloway has done," Andrew cleared his throat.

Christian sat erect in his chair; he knew all eyes would be on him.
"9:45, Sergeant Tate gets a call about a suspicious character near 44th and Michigan. Sergeant Tate responds to the call and drives to the area; here he sees Mr. Smith crouched between two bushes. Now," Andrew paused. "When Sergeant Tate arrives on the scene, he has no intention of chasing Mr. Smith. He has absolutely no intentions of drawing his weapon or having to even make an arrest. All he wants to do is talk to Mr. Smith about what he's up to; everyone would have made it home. But something went terribly wrong," Andrew spoke.

Christian looked at Keisha and could see the tears in her eyes.

Back at the prison, Raymond watched as Andrew spoke.
"Come through, man," he spoke.
"Hey, Alpha," an inmate called. "Isn't that your boy?" the inmate sat at the table with Raymond.
"Yeah, that's him. They're starting his trial today and that's the lawyer speaking."
"Man, he's got a White judge. And after killing that White boy, they ain't gonna go easy on him," the inmate spoke.
"Hush," Raymond spoke.
"*After Mr. Smith ran for the second time, Sergeant Tate chases behind him once more. Now, we already know Mr. Smith has a weapon, that's been established,*" Andrew spoke over the television.
Andrew demonstrated to the jury how Benjamin drew his weapon for the second time.

"Mr. Smith made a conscious decision to draw his weapon once more. Sergeant Tate reported that Mr. Smith had a weapon and continued the chase. Mr. Smith lost his footing and tripped over this tree root," he showed an image of the root on the screen, "and as Sergeant Tate approached, regardless of the orders to remain on his stomach with his arms and hands extended, Mr. Smith pulled out his weapon and began pulling the trigger." Andrew paced the floor again.

"Sergeant Tate had to make a long-term decision in a short amount of time; that's when you hear the deadly shot."

Andrew walked back to the desk and picked up his cup of water.

"The video does go dark; at this moment, I don't have the answers for you as to why that is, but I can guarantee you that Mr. Tate had no responsibility for that," Andrew took a sip of his water.

"Was he on the ground? Yes," Andrew continued, "but once he was down, that should have been it. Sergeant Tate saw the firearm on Mr. Smith and didn't fire a shot. He held off as much as he could, and refrained from discharging his weapon."

Christian partially spaced out as Andrew spoke to the jury.
He still couldn't picture Keisha and his child living a normal life, and it brought fear to his mind concerning their safety.

"He's lost it all," Andrew continued; Christian zoned back in. "He has this label over his head and has been stripped of his job. They've tainted this man's name and have painted a picture of him as a killer. What more could they do?" he asked rhetorically. "Bring him to court to further attempt to damage his reputation." Andrew walked away slowly. "Let this man go," he spoke softly as he sat down beside Christian.

"This is a high profile case, as you all are aware," Tracy spoke. "We're going to keep this thing rolling; I'm sure everyone wants to reach a resolution as soon as possible," she shuffled through papers. "Has all of the evidence been submitted and processed?"

"Everything has been entered from the prosecution," Judy spoke.

"All set from the defense, Your Honor," Andrew spoke as he shuffled through papers.

"Present your case," Tracy spoke.
***
Christian walked into his cell and sat down.

His mind was stuck on everything that occurred throughout the day, but one thing he couldn't erase was what Judy said: '*the defendant is no more than a killer who needs to be taken off these streets.*'

Christian shook his head.

He wondered how everyone could hail him as a hero when he was an officer, but as soon as things got rough and he had to pull the trigger, he was a criminal.

He was certain that Nanos wasn't going through this. Although Nanos was charged, as soon as the jury found him not guilty, he was able to retain his FOID card, concealed carry license, all of his police training, and he was immediately hired by a different police department; he knew it wouldn't be the case for him.

Christian stood up and punched the wall out of disgust and paced his cell. The blood dripped from his knuckles onto the floor as he shook his head. He groaned loudly.

There was a bang at his cell.

"Keep it down in there," Charles spoke with a chuckle.

Christian wanted to tell him to go to hell, but he knew it was best to remain calm and not respond.

He could hear Charles walk off and he continued to pace the floor.

"Here, boss," Raymond spoke as he passed him a t-shirt through the slot between the two cells. "Don't worry, it's clean."

Christian couldn't help but chuckle at Raymond.

"Good lookin', man," he replied.

"I was watching you in court today," Raymond spoke. "That prosecutor is tough," he spoke.

"Tell me about it," Christian shook his head. "I worked with her."

"She's the one who got me all this time," Raymond laughed. "Got me in here like I popped one in a fool. I mean, even after my confession, I still got damn near 25-to-life."

"No way," Christian spoke. "Over an armed robbery?" he asked.

"I told you, man, this isn't my first offense."

Christian shook his head as he wrapped his hand in the shirt.

"It's fucked up," Raymond added. "But," he clapped his hands together, "this is the system that we must live by."

"Unfortunately," Christian added as he finished wrapping his hand.

Raymond walked to the far end of his cell and picked up a piece of paper. "I spoke to Andrew the other day," Raymond spoke through the slot. "He gave me this piece of paper with the layout of the case," he handed the paper to Christian.

Christian pulled it through the slot and unfolded it.

"Does it look legitimate to you?" he asked.

Christian studied the paper.

"From the looks of it," Christian started, "it looks like he's going to try to plead you out on the basis that you had no other choice and were mentally unstable at the time of the robbery. And I'm not going to lie to you," he continued, "I wouldn't want to be a prosecutor against the defense, just based on what's written here."

A smirk appeared across Raymond's face.

"So, you're telling me I'm going to see my family again before I have grandchildren?" he asked.

Christian could tell Raymond was smiling.

"What Andrew wrote on this paper makes it a strong possibility," Christian finished.

Christian folded the paper and slid it back through the slot.

Raymond placed it back on his bed.

"I'm certain of it," Christian added.

"If I could, I would give you some dap right now," Raymond spoke with a scoff. "But I got you tomorrow."

Christian laughed.

"Let's get some shut-eye, bro," Raymond spoke.

"Cool," Christian spoke as he closed his slot.

Christian walked over to his bed and sat down.

He heard a loud buzz and the cell door slid open. He saw other cell doors open as well.

"What the fuck?" he spoke aloud.

He saw some of the inmates leave their cells and he walked to his door. He poked his head out and saw the door open that separated the maximum-security inmates from the other level.

"Oh shit," Christian spoke as he saw some of the inmates running towards the door.

Raymond walked over to his cell door and looked out.

The inmates walked through the doors and some held shanks that were made in the prison. Raymond saw they were headed for Christian's cell. The inmates started jogging as they got closer to Christian's cell and Raymond stepped outside. They started yelling and shouting as they approached.

"Stay low, boss," he spoke as he stood in front of Christian's door.

"I can't let you handle them alone," Christian spoke.

He ensured his hand was wrapped tightly with the shirt and walked to the door.

Charles was the first officer to enter the hall and he led many officers to control the inmates.

"Get on the ground," they each shouted as they ran in with assault rifles.

The inmates who held shanks dropped them to the floor and laid on the floor.

Raymond saw Charles leading the other officers and quickly returned to his cell; Christian sat down on his bed.

As the other officers were controlling the inmates, Charles walked directly to Christian's cell.

Charles looked inside and smirked at Christian.

"Light's out!" he shouted at Christian. "Gotta keep you niggers in line," he spoke in a low tone.

Christian stared at Charles but said nothing.

Charles walked over to Raymond's cell and pulled him out.

"Come on, man!" Raymond exclaimed.

Christian heard Raymond and rose from his bed. He walked to his door and saw that Charles had Raymond on the floor.

"He didn't even do shit," Christian spoke.

Charles glanced up and spoke to Christian.

"Do I have to pull my gun?" he shouted. "Back to your cell."

"This is bullshit," Christian spoke. "Get off of him."

"Back to your fuckin' cell," Charles spoke louder.

"Chris, it's cool," Raymond spoke. "I got this, brotha'."

Raymond didn't want anything to potentially interfere with Christian getting out of jail.

Christian returned to his cell and paced the floor.

A few seconds later, the shouting ceased and the cell doors were closing; the inmates returned to their cells.

"Don't let that shit happen again," Charles projected. He established a presence in front of Christian's cell. "You better get some rest, young lady," he spoke in a low tone to Christian. "You have court in the morning."

Christian didn't release his glare at Charles. Charles exited the hall and Christian opened the slot to talk to Raymond.

"You good?"

"Yeah, boss. I'm straight," Raymond responded. "There's nothing that can be done to affect me in here."

Christian shook his head.

"I feel like he was just responsible for that," he admitted.

"Why do you say that?" Raymond asked.

"Just a vibe I'm feeling," Christian spoke. "Dude smirked at me, and I wouldn't put it past him to do something like that."

"Keep an eye on him," Raymond spoke. "But do *not* let him affect you getting out of here," he stressed.

"It's not in my plans," Christian expressed. "And you don't let him affect you either."

"We got a deal," Raymond spoke before closing the slot.

Christian walked over to his bed and pulled a picture of Keisha from his jumpsuit.

"I love you, babe. I'll be out of here soon," he spoke to the image.
He kissed the picture and held it to his chest.
Christian closed his eyes and soon he was asleep.

9

Christian wore his suit and stood next to Andrew as Judy spoke to the jury.

"A straight 'A' student; he'd never been in trouble with the law, not even as much as a parking ticket. "You're meaning to tell me that this young man fled from police and pulled out his firearm on someone he *knew* was a police officer?" Judy made eye contact with Christian. Judy quickly looked away.
She refocused her attention on the jury.
"Put yourself in his position," she continued. "It's late at night and you suddenly see a large man speak to you in a gruff voice and he asks you what you're up to. You would run too," she scoffed. "Now, once the defendant verbally identified himself as police and with the siren lights, yes, some may argue that he should have stopped. But 18-year-old Benjamin Smith," she made sure to throw his age in her argument, "was in an area that was known for a string of robberies and African American males impersonating police officers. Can't tell what's real from what's fake anymore," she concluded as she returned to the center of the room.

"Your Honor, we would like to call William Longon to the stand," Judy spoke as William rose from his chair.
William was a middle-aged Caucasian male who glared at Christian

as he made his way to the bench. Christian noticed the slight limp the man had.

As William walked past Christian, Christian felt as though a cold air followed him.

William was sworn in and sat in the witness chair.

"Mr. Longon, how long did you know Benjamin?" Judy asked.

"I knew Benjamin for roughly three years," William spoke in what sounded like a monotone to Christian.

"And what was your relationship to Mr. Smith?" Judy questioned.

"I was his counselor," he started before clearing his throat. "He was a good kid."

"Mr. Longon, did Benjamin ever speak to you regarding any issues or concerns he had in his community?" Judy asked.

"Can you elaborate?" he asked.

"Sure," she started. "Did he ever talk to you about injustices regarding police brutality?"

"It's a hot topic nationally," William answered, "but not within our school."

Andrew took notes on his notepad as William spoke.

"Specifically, how about the State of Florida versus Nanos case?"

"We actually did discuss that in passing, as did many other students with myself."

"How about harassment from law enforcement?" Judy questioned.

"Objection, Your Honor," Andrew interjected.

"Withdrawn," Judy smirked while looking directly at William. "Mr. Longon, what classes were Benjamin enrolled in?" she continued.

"The usual," William replied. "Math, English, Social Science, Economics, Politics."

"Any extracurriculars?" she asked.

"He was big on studying the Black culture," William spoke after a moment of silence. "So he was taking up hip-hop dance, African-American history, and he was even studying A-A-L-E."

There were small murmurs from the jury.

"Sounds like a student who wanted to be informed. Can you inform us as to what A-A-L-E is?" Judy asked.

"African-Americans in Law Enforcement," William answered.

The jurors looked at one another and nodded.

Andrew looked down and silently sorted through the papers in the envelope.

"And what kind of things were taught in A-A-L-E?" she quickly asked.

"Where do I begin?" William chuckled. "Students can learn about the first African American lawyers and judges, first African American police officers, how Blacks influenced the laws across America," William boasted. "It really sets a positive image and gives the minority the praise they deserve."

Christian felt like giving an outburst at William's comments and Andrew noticed this.

Andrew put his hand on Christian's shoulder to tell him to calm down.

"So, Benjamin sounds like he was really intrigued at how the African American culture made a difference in this country."

"Indeed, he was," William replied. "I haven't met a kid as focused and determined as him."

William scanned the room and found Benjamin's parents.

"Mr. and Mrs. Smith, my condolences to you for your loss."

William picked up a tissue, turned his head, and blew his nose.

"Excuse me," he spoke to the court.

"Mr. Longon, it's reported that you've shadowed Mr. Smith before, is this correct?"

"Yes," William replied.

"Please, tell the court what a typical day of following behind Benjamin was like."

"Mr. Smith was an interesting young man," William answered. "All of his teachers seemed to love him and he was very popular amongst his peers," he was proud of Benjamin and it showed. "He was very interactive and conversational in class, and the teachers appreciated his contributions. Very, very respectful young man," William finished.

"Thank you, Mr. Longon. No further questions, Your Honor," Judy walked back to her desk.

Andrew straightened his tie and approached the bench with his notepad and manilla folder.

"William Longon, is it?" he asked.

William started to respond but Andrew quickly continued.

"How long have you been a counselor at Rapier Heights?" Andrew asked.

"Roughly 6 years," William replied.

"And what's the student-teacher ratio there?" Andrew asked.

"About a 5-to-1 ratio. It's not that bad," he chuckled as he looked at the jurors.

"Mr. Longon, I've done my research on your school and have printed out the following," he handed him a piece of paper from the folder.

William studied the page and his cheeks turned a rosy color.

"Mr. Longon, can you tell the jury what you're looking at?" Andrew asked as he looked at Judy with a slight smirk.

Judy glared at him.

"Rapier Heights' demographics," William spoke.

"Okay, Mr. Longon, and according to the report generated in December 2018, a-k-a last year, how many teachers do you all have at Rapier Heights?" Andrew slowly paced the floor.

"81 teachers," William responded. "Twenty-six security guards, eleven counselors, three secretaries, one principal, and one assistant principal," he continued.

"Thank you for reading that off," Andrew replied. "Now would you do me a favor and read off the nationalities of the faculty?"

"Objection, Your Honor," Judy projected. "Relevance?"

"Where is this going, Mr. Brownstone?" Tracy asked.

"This is going to provide insight to Rapier Heights and their curriculum," Andrew calmly replied.

"This better be good," Tracy replied. "Overruled. Answer the question, Mr. Longon."

William sighed.

"According to this report, 70% of the staff at Rapier Heights are of Caucasian descent. 10% are of Hispanic descent, 11% are Asian, 5% are Middle Eastern, and 4% are African-American."

There were murmurs from the jurors and the audience.

"And what about the student demographics?" Andrew continued immediately following William's reading.

William looked around as if he were looking for an escape.

"93% of the students are Caucasian, 5% are Hispanic, and 2% are labeled as other."

"Other?" Andrew asked. "Care to elaborate?"

William let out a small sigh; not audible to the jury, but Andrew could tell he didn't want to continue.

Judy could see how uncomfortable William was, but she didn't have anything to object to.

"The report lists other as any race that isn't Caucasian and Hispanic. The numbers reported were too low for statistical data. In this case, 'Other' represents students of Middle Eastern, Asian, and African-American descent."

Andrew looked at the jurors.

"So, in a school that has a diverse curriculum, you would think the diversity would be amongst the students and faculty as well," Andrew spoke.

"Objection, Your Honor. Speculation," Judy responded.

"Sustained," Tracy responded. "Do you have a question, Mr. Brownstone?"

Andrew gave a slight nod.

"I just find it a little concerning that a school with a 2% African-American faculty and less than 2% student population has courses on African-American law," he slightly shook his head. "Mr. Longon, can you read the breakdown of each role of the faculty members by demographic?" Andrew added.

William displayed his frustration.

"What?" he chuckled. "Do you want to say how many of our faculty are Black?"

Andrew looked at the jury for their reactions.

"We have three Black teachers at Rapier Heights and three Black security guards," William spoke with disgust.

"So, out of 123 faculty members in the school, there are only 6 African American administrators?" Andrew spoke with emphasis to give a dramatic effect.

William was silent.

The jurors looked at each other and wrote down the statistics.

After a few moments, Christian took a sip of water and Andrew proceeded. "I was able to obtain a list of the courses taken by Benjamin, and I cross-referenced it with the list of courses offered by the school. There isn't a course titled 'A-A-L-E' or 'African-Americans in Law Enforcement' on the list," Andrew continued. "Does A-A-L-E potentially have a different name?" Andrew looked at the list of classes.

William's cheeks turned red again and looked at Judy.

"Ah, I'm right here," he shook his head as he blocked the view of Judy.

"Well, it was originally given the title 'N-L-E'," William spoke.

Andrew raised his eyebrow.

"N-L-E? What does that acronym stand for? And why was it changed to A-A-L-E?" he asked.

William mumbled.

Christian leaned forward to hear what William had said.

"I'm sorry, Mr. Longon, can you speak louder so the jury can hear you?" Andrew asked.

"Your Honor, I object!" Judy objected again. "If my witness has already given the name of the course, why does the past title matter?" she asked.

"Credibility," Andrew replied.

It was obvious that he was getting annoyed with Judy and her objections.

"How are you going to list a name as one of the classes, but the name provided isn't what's on the registrar? It doesn't add up," Andrew recited.

"I'll allow it," Tracy replied.

"N-L-E: it stands for Negroes in Law Enforcement," William projected. Numerous murmurs could be heard from the jurors and across the courtroom.

Beads of sweat formed across William's face and Benjamin's parents looked around the room.

The judge slammed her gavel and called for order.
Once the courtroom silenced, Andrew scoffed and spoke.
"Negroes in Law Enforcement," he started, "seems a little interesting that a predominantly Caucasian school has a class with this title."
"Well, the controversial name is the reason the name has been changed," William tried to clear up the confusion.
"Pending a name change," Andrew interjected. "As far as the Department of Education is concerned, the name is still *Negroes in Law Enforcement*," Andrew ensured to stress the name for the court; the audience, the jurors, the lawyers, and prosecutors, as well as the cameras.
Judy wrote a note on her notepad as she watched on. A look of disgust was on her face.

"Please, tell me about the conversation you had with Benjamin regarding the State of Florida versus Nanos case."
William swallowed air. William looked at Judy to object.
"Your Honor, what does this have to do with this case?" Judy blurted.
"The cases are the same; the roles have just been reversed. So, it would be valuable for the jurors to know how Mr. Smith reacted to Nanos walking free to compare it with the outcome of his situation."
"Ms. Holloway, you've had quite a few objections and this is only the first witness," Tracy reply. "Overruled," she finished.
William waited a few moments before picking up his cup of water.

"I spoke to Benjamin the day following the verdict; it seems like everyone in the school was discussing it," he started after clearing his throat. "When Benjamin came into my office, he had a huge smile on his face," William shook his head.
Andrew wanted to smile, but he refrained from doing so.
"I asked him what was going on," William continued, "he told me he was kind of excited because of the verdict. Nanos was walking free and he was ecstatic because he truly believed the shooting was justified."

Andrew sucked his teeth as the jurors expressed concern.

"So, let me get this straight," he started, "a White police officer shooting and killing an unarmed Black male was justified?"

"Objection, Your Honor," Judy interjected once more.

"Sustained," Tracy replied.

"Let me ask you this," Andrew continued. "In your opinion, let's say Benjamin was here. He knew he was armed and aimed his weapon at Sergeant Tate; do you think he would he say the shooting by Tate was justified?"

William was silent and Andrew walked away.

"No further questions, Your Honor."

Andrew walked back to his seat and Judy rose to her feet.

"Damage control," Andrew whispered to Christian.

"No rebuttal, Your Honor," Judy spoke. "I am sorry for your loss, Mr. Longon. I'm sure Rapier Heights will be an empty vessel without Benjamin's smiling face."

"You may step down, Mr. Longon," Tracy instructed.

William rose from the chair and stepped down from the stand.
***

Christian walked over and sat at the bench that Raymond resided.

"Where'd you find your lawyer?" he exclaimed.

He showed his excitement and greeted Christian with a fist bump.

"Known him for years," Christian replied as he adjusted his t-shirt.

"Man," Raymond shook his head. "You look so different in these jail clothes," he spoke to Christian.

Christian caught a glimpse of himself in the mirror across the room and was a little ashamed at the image he saw.

"Man, I can't wait until this shit is over," Christian spoke in disgust.

"Look man," Raymond spoke, "this is just a minor setback. As you know, this country isn't meant for us to succeed, even though we built it."

Christian chuckled lightly.

"Yeah, you're right, man," Christian agreed.

Raymond rose to his feet.

"Where you headed?" Christian asked.

"Headed this weight room, my guy. You coming?"

Christian studied Raymond before responding.

"Yeah, I guess you didn't get that size from just fuckin' around," he chuckled.

Christian followed Raymond to the fitness area of the jail.

Christian looked at the worn-down equipment and shook his head.

"This is what they have you all using?"

"Yeah, man," Raymond spoke. "It's not much, but it gets the heart racing."

Looking at the state of the equipment, Christian knew something had to be done.

"They should have some better stuff than this," he lifted the weight.

"We've been trying to get more stuff in, but nothing has changed,"

Raymond walked over to the bench and took off his shirt.

He wiped the bench off with his shirt before speaking.

He laid his shirt on the bench.

"Spot me," he finished.

Christian walked over to the bench, which had a bar with 100 pounds on each end.

"Come on, my guy," Christian joked, "you don't need me for this," he referenced Raymond's physique.

Raymond laughed.

"I'm glad you feel that way, but I need for you to spot me," he assured him.

"Just following the rules," Raymond laid on his shirt and put his hands in the center of the bar.

Christian chuckled and put hands under the bar.

"Whenever you're ready," he spoke.

Raymond lifted the bar and lowered it to his chest.

"You're going to have to tell me about how Andrew pulled that shit off today," Raymond spoke as he raised and lowered the bar.

"Man, I wish I knew," Christian spoke. "That shit was genius," he admitted. "I think what really took the jury was when he asked if William thought that Benjamin would have justified this shooting."

"Let's not forget about the school's curriculum," Raymond spoke as he exhaled.

"Man, and then he was able to cross with some of Benjamin's classmates and teachers. None of them really helped the case," Christian chuckled lightly.

"I saw that shit. Judy had the nerve to keep objecting even though she knew Benjamin was in the wrong."

"That's what prosecutors do," Christian admitted. "If things aren't going our way, we object to divert attention," he shrugged.

Raymond looked at Christian as he continued to lift; he didn't utter a word.

Moments later, Christian and Raymond were leaving the fitness area; both were covered in sweat.

"Good workout, bro," Raymond spoke to Christian as he patted his back.

"You too, man," Christian replied. "First time in that center; I've been just doing pushups and situps to keep fit."

Charles saw the two walking and bumped Christian's arm.

"Come on, man, what the hell?" Christian exclaimed.

"Shit, my bad," Charles spoke. "Looks like you need to watch where you're walking."

"Or *you* need to watch where *you're* walking," Christian retaliated as he stepped closer to Charles.

Raymond saw Charles put his hand near his utility belt.

"It's not even worth it, man," Raymond spoke to Christian.

"Listen to your friend, nigger," Charles spoke.

"You know what, you got a smart ass mouth," Christian retaliated, "and you talk too much. That shit is going to be your demise," he argued.

Raymond and Christian both walked in the opposite direction of Charles.

"I'm not about to be playing this game with him," Christian shrugged his shoulders; anger filled his body. "He thinks because he's an officer of the jail that he's above everyone else?"

"Yeah, but C, you're a cop. You know you have to play the rules to advance," Raymond spoke. "It's just the way it is," he continued to walk with Christian.

Christian gave thought to what he was saying but continued the walk.

"I'll admit it, since I've partnered with you in here, I've gained a lot more confidence and I feel like I've learned a lot, but don't forget I've been in here numerous times and I know how this game works, especially with these guards," Raymond responded in a low tone. "It's often best to move in silence, trust me."

"You're right," Christian spoke after a few seconds of silence.

The hallway seemed longer than it was when Christian and Raymond had previously walked down; it was so quiet that Christian could have sworn he was hearing footsteps behind them.

"Andrew is supposed to be coming up here," Christian spoke. "He's meeting with me, but I'm going to see if he will also meet with you."

"Maybe he can jam them up for me the way he did for you," Raymond chuckled.

"He tells the truth," Christian shrugged, "and as they say: the truth will set you free."

"Yeah, man."

As they got back to the center hall, Christian was approached by a prison guard.

"Christian Tate, your lawyer is here," the guard spoke.

Christian shook hands with Raymond and followed the guard.

He followed the guard to the secluded room where Andrew sat.

The guard left the room and Christian sat down.

"That shit that you did was genius," he spoke with excitement.

Andrew and Christian did their handshake.

"No doubt, man. My job is to get you out of here and back to your wife, whom I see has a baby on the way," Andrew smiled. "Congrats, man."

"She's due any day now, and it's kind of crazy that I won't be able to be there for the birth of my child," Christian shook his head.

"But we're going to get you out before her first birthday," Andrew promised. "We just have to stay focused. After Judy saw what I did today, she's taking notes and is going to be attacking from every angle."

"What's your biggest concern?" Christian asked.

"To be honest," Andrew spoke, "it's got to be the video. I know you and I know your heart, so I'm not worried about defending you, but I'm not positive I know how to defend the video when Judy decides to bring it up."

"The truth," Christian replied. "I have nothing to hide, and as you said, you know me and my heart."

"Yeah, but we need to make the jury know you and your heart. The fact that most of them are White just means we have to work that much harder," Andrew replied. "You're going to be the last witness that I call to the stand."

Christian raised his eyebrow.

"You have no choice but to take the stand," Andrew continued.

"I didn't expect anything less," Christian replied. "The jury has to hear directly from me."

"I'll keep working to figure things out with the video," Andrew responded. "There has to be an answer for the visual cutting out."

"If you need anything from me, let me know," Christian sat erect. "Have you spoken with Raymond recently?" he asked as he changed subjects.

"Not recently," Andrew answered as he realized Christian changed subjects. "Been diverting all of my energy to getting you out of here," he emphasized.

"I would like for you to meet with him today. I made him a promise that you would work with him to get him out of here," Christian replied.

Andrew sighed.

"Focus, Christian," he spoke. "Let's get you out of here and then we can worry about everything else."

Christian looked at Andrew sternly.

"Man, that's not what we're about," Christian spoke with a sense of authority. "You know that as well as I do. We help each other," Christian finished.

Andrew sighed.

"Is he waiting for me or something?" he asked.

"I told him I would ask you to speak with him after speaking with me," Christian uttered.

Andrew shook his head.

"Okay, cool. I'll talk to him," Andrew conceded.

Christian shook hands with Andrew before continuing the conversation about his case.

"As far as the video is concerned," Andrew projected, "I'm going to dig deeper, but when it's time for you to take the stand, you look those jurors in the eyes and you show them who Sergeant Christian Tate is. Show them that you're not the monster the prosecution is making you out to be." Andrew adjusted his tie. "I don't know when I'll be calling you to the stand because I'm not sure how long their witnesses will take, but just be ready."

"I'll be ready," Christian spoke with confidence.

"From here on out, we're moving fast. The witnesses will be pouring in and you know they want to put you away. Finish your list of people that we should contact and subpoena to give you a strong counter-argument," Andrew looked at the clock on the wall.

"Okay," Christian spoke.

"And I'll keep the cross-examinations hitting hard," Andrew shook his hand. "Now go on and send your homie in here," Andrew chuckled. "We don't want these guards to lock everything down."

Christian rose to his feet and the guard entered the room.

"Can you bring Raymond Farris in, please?" Andrew spoke as he rose to his feet.

The guard nodded his head.

He escorted Christian from the room and took him back to the dormitory.

"He's waiting for you, Boss," Christian spoke to Raymond.

"Good looking, man," Raymond replied as the guard escorted him to Andrew.

Christian sat at the table and thought about Keisha, his unborn child, who they should call to defend his name, and, to his surprise, Benjamin.

"Why did you do it?" Christian asked aloud as he thought of Benjamin.

10

"Ladies and gentlemen of the jury," Judy started, "Mr. Oliver Warren is a private pathologist who performed the autopsy on Benjamin Smith. He has performed multiple autopsies and has studied numerous murder cases and will be providing his feedback based on his findings. Now, I want to warn you that while questioning Mr. Warren, we will be displaying some pretty graphic and potentially upsetting images; just a fair warning. At this time, if that will bother you, to avoid outbursts, we ask that you leave the courtroom."

Oliver rose to his feet and walked to the witness stand. None of the congregation exited, not even Benjamin's parents.
Once he sat, he was sworn in.
"Good morning, Mr. Warren," Judy spoke as she greeted her witness.
"Good morning," he replied.
"Mr. Warren, thank you for taking time out of your busy schedule. We're not going to hold you for too long," Judy hurried.
"Take your time," Oliver spoke as he motioned his hand.
"Mr. Warren, when you first started this autopsy, is there anything that immediately stood out to you?" Judy asked as she walked towards the board and referred to the autopsy images of Benjamin's body.

"If you look at tag number one, he stated as he used his laser pointer to highlight the section he was referring to, "this really stood out to me."
The laser was aimed at the scratches on Benjamin's arms and legs.
"Mr. Smith sustained scratches to his torso, as well as his arms and legs."
"And why did this stand out to you?" Judy asked.
"It is reported that Mr. Smith fled from the defendant before pulling out his gun. It was never mentioned that they engaged in a scuffle."
"Ah," Judy corrected him, "but the defendant did confirm that he had to tase Mr. Smith. Couldn't these injuries have been from Mr. Smith returning to the Earth from the jolt of electricity in his body?"
"That would make sense," Oliver spoke, "but it's reported that Mr. Smith fell on his back when he collapsed from the fence. So," Oliver cleared his throat, "the injuries should be on his back, and as you can see, "he pointed the laser to the image of Benjamin's back, "there are no injuries to his back at all with the exception of the exit point of the bullet."

Theresa teared as she looked at the images. His father put his arm around her and the court officer took the box of tissue over to her.

"Is there anything else that stood out to you?" Judy asked.
"Not necessarily, not at first sight," Oliver spoke. "When I was contacted to perform the autopsy and I received the body and did a few tests, I was a little concerned."
"Why is that?" Judy asked.
"After running tests, I found that Benjamin's heart didn't stop until about five-to-ten minutes after the bullet entered his chest. His heart continued to pump blood; granted, it was pumping faster, but his body was keeping everything regulated."
"So, what are you saying?" Judy asked. "That Benjamin could have survived the shot?"
"Precisely," Warren spoke with confidence. "The additional pressure to his heart from the C.P.R. caused it to pump faster and harder, which caused him to lose blood at a quicker rate."
"But C.P.R. is supposed to save lives, isn't it?" she raised her eyebrows.

"Normally, but in this case, the heart was beating rapidly. Benjamin's heart was already pumping quickly from the adrenaline of the chase and the volt of electricity that passed through him. The only thing that would have needed to be done was to apply pressure to the wound."
Andrew shook his head.
"Had that been done, Benjamin would have been fine."
"So, are you arguing that Christian Tate is the cause of death, two times over?" she looked at the jury.
"Objection, Your Honor," Andrew enunciated.
"Sustained," Tracy replied.

Judy nodded her head and proceeded to speak.
"So, Mr. Warren, what exactly are you saying with this information?"
"Benjamin Smith survived the initial gunshot wound," he adjusted his seating. "He didn't transition until C.P.R. was administered. It caused his heart to beat faster and lose blood at a quicker rate."

Judy looked at the court.
"Was there anything else that you found that could have contributed to his death? Ligature marks?"
"Objection, Your Honor," Andrew spoke. "Leading the witness."
"Withdrawn," Judy immediately replied. "Mr. Warren, is there anything else you can tell us about Benjamin's death?" Judy asked as she exhausted her questions.
"Nothing else that really stood out," Oliver shook his head.
"Thank you, Mr. Warren," Judy walked back to her desk and took a seat.

Andrew slowly rose from his chair and approached the witness stand.
"Sorry we had to drag you from your business, Mr. Warren," he started.
Oliver shook his head.
"Mr. Warren, you said you found it concerning that Mr. Smith had scrapes and scratches on his arms and legs," Andrew spoke.
"In my opinion, it was," Oliver replied.
"Well, there was definitely sort of something that happened for him to have the scrapes," Oliver chuckled.

"How about tripping? Do you think that could have caused it?" Andrew asked.

Oliver thought before answering.

"Because, that's what happened," Andrew continued before Oliver could speak. "Mr. Smith fled from my client and in the process of running, he tripped over a root; hence the reason for his clothes being stained and him having small debris from the ground on him."

"I suppose that's possible," Oliver replied.

"*That's because that's what happened,*" Christian thought.

"I have one more concern," Andrew spoke as he stood erect. "You're saying the C.P.R. administered on Benjamin is what killed him?" Andrew asked.

"Objection; speculation," Judy spoke.

"Your Honor, I'm just trying to get some clarification," Andrew immediately bit back.

Tracy thought for a moment and proceeded.

"Overruled," she replied. "Proceed, Mr. Warren."

"After my analysis, yes," Oliver answered Andrew's question.

"So, Benjamin would have been better off if my client didn't do anything after the shooting?" Andrew paced the floor.

"If that's how you want to put it," Oliver replied.

"If that's the way I want to put it?" Andrew asked. "That's what you're saying," he replied. "Your argument is that Benjamin would have survived had C.P.R. not been performed."

"*No, he would still be alive had he complied,*" Christian thought.

"All I'm doing is reporting my findings," Oliver shrugged.

Andrew decided to switch the subjects.

"Mr. Warren, how many autopsies have you performed in your career?"

Oliver scratched his chin.

"My office has performed over 1500 autopsies over a seven-year span. I've personally performed about 300 out of those 1500."

"How large is your company?"

"We have roughly 50 employees."

"And out of those 1500 autopsies, how many have been performed on people of color?" Andrew questioned.

"Objection, Your Honor," Judy spoke.

"I have a reason for asking the question," Andrew spoke as he tried to think of the reasoning.

Tracy raised her eyebrows. Before she could respond to the objection, Oliver answered.

"It's hard to give an approximate number but I would guess around 200 of our cases have been of your pe—people of Color," he corrected himself.

Andrew heard the error and could hear a slight reaction by the jurors.

"That's interesting that you say that," Andrew walked back to the desk near Christian.

He pulled a piece of paper from the folder.

Andrew read the paper as he walked back over to the witness stand.

"Statistics from *your* company's website show that only fifty of the autopsies performed have been on African-Americans," Andrew heard slight murmurs from the crowd. "And it further lists the description of the company as a 'firm that performs the autopsy services for those who have suffered injustice. We are going to make America great again, one autopsy at a time'."

Oliver raised his eyebrow and looked at Julie.

She looked at him with disappointment.

"So, which is inaccurate, the site, or your verbal word?"

Oliver looked at Andrew in his eyes as if he were trying to pierce his soul.

"All I can say is that I stand by my word. I know how many cases I have done and how many bodies were Black."

"How many bodies were Black," Andrew repeated in disbelief. "*Wow,*" he mouthed.

He heard murmurs from the jurors.

Andrew smirked at Oliver as he could see puzzled looks on the juror's faces.

"No further questions, Your Honor," Andrew walked back to his seat.

Judy shook her head before speaking.

"Thank you, Mr. Warren."

Oliver stepped down and Judy rose to her feet.

"Your Honor, the prosecution calls Patricia Young to the stand."

As Patricia rose to her feet and walked to the stand, Judy continued.

"Patricia was Benjamin's best friend and was the last one to talk to him on the phone, just moments before the fatal shooting."

Patricia stared at Christian as she was sworn in and rolled her eyes.

"Patricia, I am so sorry for your loss," Judy spoke. "I know this is going to be hard for you, but take your time if you need it," she sympathized.

Patricia nodded her head.

"Thank you."

"How long did you know Mr. Smith?"

Judy's angle was to tug at the juror's emotions by bringing his best friend to testify, but Andrew had no worries and knew how to handle the situation.

"I knew Benjamin for fifteen years," she cleared her throat.

"That's a long time," Judy replied. "How would you describe your relationship to him?"

"Benjamin and I were best friends, although I think we both wanted it to be more than that," Patricia sniffled. "We went everywhere together, with the exception of the day of the tragic shooting."

"But, you were on the phone with him, correct?"

"Yes," Patricia adjusted her posture.

"Can you run us down the timeline of everything that happened from when you were on the phone with him leading up to that fateful moment?"

"Well," she inhaled sharply. "Around 8:30, I called Benjamin; I believe he was heading home to relax after class."

Andrew wrote on the notepad as Patricia spoke. He sifted through the folder; searching diligently to break the case.

"He told me that he was going to take a different route home, since it was a shortcut. Well, Benjamin told me he'd dropped his keys in the bushes and I could hear him searching for them. He laughed as he looked for them in the rain; everything was muddy and it was making his search much more difficult, but that was Ben for you; always making light out of a situation. Suddenly I heard a siren approach and a man called to him."

"Did you hear what the man shouted?" Judy asked.

"I remember the moment vividly. 'What's going on?' is what he asked," Patricia continued. "Benjamin asked me what he should do because he felt scared. He couldn't swear if it was truly a police officer and he knew he had his firearm on him. Without thinking, I panicked, and since I panicked, he panicked and ran. I wish I hadn't panicked," Patricia pulled a sheet a Kleenex from the box in front of her.

"Take your time," Judy sympathized.

Patricia continued.

"When Ben ran, he didn't hang up the phone. I could hear his feet as they hit the ground and as they crunched the leaves. I heard the defendant shout 'Miami P-D, freeze' and 'if you don't stop, you will be tased, but I believe Ben felt he was bluffing and feared for his life. I heard a jingling noise before I heard Ben scream," Patricia closed her eyes and let out a few tears. "I can remember myself saying 'Ben, Babe, Benji' desperately trying to get his attention and I could hear footsteps walking and crunching the leaves and sticks. He asked Benji 'why you running?' and I heard Benji reply "eff you."

"I'm assuming 'Benji is the nickname' you gave the late Benjamin Smith," Judy chose her words carefully as the jury looked on.

"Yes," Patricia answered. "Once he said," Patricia stuttered as to not utter the word in court on accident, "what he said," she slightly blushed, "I heard the man say 'sit down' and I heard another jingling noise. It was different than the one I'd previously heard. And then I heard another noise and the man shouted 'drop your weapon'. From that point, I knew things were going to take a turn for the worse," she looked at the jury.

"Miss Young, what else did you hear?"

"I heard Ben running and I heard 'Miami P-D'. Benji was breathing heavily and I heard another fall. The last thing I remember hearing before the call ended was a gunshot and the approacher shouting 'shots fired'."

Patricia wiped her eyes with a piece of Kleenex.

"I know this is hard for you and you've been through a lot, so I want to say 'thank you' for coming today," Judy walked back to her desk.
Andrew looked at the jurors and saw tears in some of their eyes.
"Shit," he whispered.
He knew what he had to do.
Andrew approached the bench with his notepad and pieces of paper from the folder.
"Miss Young, you stated that Benjamin decided to take an alternative route home. Why did he decide to take a new route on this particular day?" Andrew asked.
"As I stated," she inhaled sharply, "he said it was a shortcut."
"A shortcut from school?" Andrew asked inquisitively.
Patricia raised an eyebrow and he placed a piece of paper in front of her.

He walked over to the smartboard and loaded the map.
"When my client apprehended the subject, he was on 44th Ct. and Michigan Ave. But the high school is on 47th and Pine Tree Drive and Benjamin lived right off of Alton Road and North Bay Road," Andrew spoke. "Now, according to this information, that means that Benjamin went further south than he would have needed to go, and that doesn't seem like much of a shortcut to me," he finished.
Patricia was silent.
"Perhaps he made another stop?" Andrew suggested.
"Objection, Your Honor," Judy interjected. "Leading the witness."
"I'll rephrase," Andrew replied. "Patricia, did Benjamin mention to you that he was making another stop before going home?"
Christian leaned forward.
"No. No he did not," Patricia answered with attitude.

It had never clicked before, but the area that Benjamin was killed was the same area that Sterling was killed.

"Could it be that Benjamin went to the convenience store located a block-and-a-half away before he was apprehended by Christian?"
Patricia looked at him.
"Ironically, Sterling Wallace visited the exact same convenience store before *that* unfateful night."
"Objection, Your Honor!" Judy shouted.
"Withdrawn," Andrew smirked as the jurors murmured.
He knew they'd heard his comment and they couldn't unhear it.
"Patricia, are you aware that security cameras at the convenience store have Benjamin on camera, moments before the shooting?"
Patricia's eyes widened.
"Yep, it turns out he's a fan of hot chips, Brisk Iced Tea, Nerds, and,"
Andrew placed a picture in front of Patricia, "racism." He displayed the image on the board.
It was a picture of Benjamin and he appeared to be shouting at the cashier.
"The picture can't speak, but I just want to point out that's an African-American cashier that Benjamin is shouting at."
"How can you tell what they are talking about through a picture?" Patricia rolled her eyes. "Maybe the cashier said or did something offensive to Ben," she shrugged her shoulders.
Andrew smirked.
"I would like for the court to pay attention to the board. I have a video I would like to show," he walked away from the bench and to the monitor.
"Your Honor," Judy interrupted, "has this been entered into evidence?" she asked.
"Actually, it has," Andrew answered for the judge. "Exhibit 3.5A. Look at your notes."
Judy looked at her notes and her cheeks turned red.

Tracy nodded her head for Andrew to continue.
He pressed play on the board and the video clip started.

"This clip was obtained directly from the convenience store and has not been enhanced, modified, or altered in any way."

The congregation saw Benjamin enter the store and saw him walk through the aisles of the store.

"*Can I help you?*" the convenience store clerk asked.

"*Help your damn self,*" Benjamin replied with disgust.

Benjamin collected his items as he spoke on the phone.

"It's assumed that Benjamin was talking to Miss Young, considering she was the last call he made and the call lasted for thirty-five minutes and sixteen seconds," Andrew narrated.

Benjamin walked to the front of the store.

"*Did you find everything okay?*" the clerk asked.

"*Is there a reason you're still talking to me?*" Benjamin shouted at the man.

"*I apologize if I said or did anything to offend you,*" the clerk spoke, "*just trying to make sure your night is going well.*"

"*You know what would be real helpful?*" Benjamin scowled.

The clerk looked at Benjamin.

"*If you and all your other colored friends would take your black asses back to Africa,*" Benjamin finished.

The jurors were shocked at his statement behavior.

"*Excuse me?*" the clerk spoke as he maintained his composure.

"*I said what I said. Hurry up and ring my shit up,*" Benjamin hurried.

The clerk didn't utter another word. When the total displayed on the register, he stared at Benjamin.

"*Hello?*" Benjamin taunted. "*Cat got your tongue or something?*" he asked.

"*These folks got a lot of shit to say but can't read or write,*" he laughed into the phone.

He dropped the exact change on the counter before walking to the exit with his items in his hand.

"*You're lucky that I'm at work right now,*" the clerk spoke. "*If you want to see what it's about, we can discuss after I get off,*" the clerk shrugged his shoulders.

"*You got yourself a date, Buddy,*" Benjamin spoke before walking out of the store.

Andrew pressed stop on the video recording and walked back over to Patricia.

"Some choice words, there," Andrew scoffed.

"What's your point in showing that?" Patricia questioned.

"Your 'Benji' had a lot of hostility and hatred in his heart that night," Andrew paced the floor slowly.

"Relevance, Your Honor," Judy shouted; she never lifted her head from the paper her eyes were focused on.

"Get to the point, Mr. Brownstone," Tracy projected.

"My point is that we are here trying Mr. Tate for murder, yet Benjamin Smith was seen just moments before the deadly shooting, speaking pugnaciously to a clerk, who just so happened to be the same skin tone as my client."

Christian clasped his hands together and sat back in the chair.

"No further questions, Your Honor," Andrew walked back to Christian and sat down.

***

Raymond greeted Christian with a handshake as he entered the hall.

"Mr. Superstar. I see you winning this trial," he emitted a small laugh.

"I don't know about that," he laughed. "But I will give Andrew his props. He's busting ass and creating so many holes; things I wouldn't have even thought to bring up."

"That's why he's the lawyer," Raymond turned and stretched.

Christian could hear the crack as Raymond rotated his body.

"I spoke with him regarding my case and he said he's building a strong case to get me out, maybe even weeks after you get out," excitement was in Raymond's voice. "He said it may not even have to go to trial."

"That's perfect news, Boss. I can't wait to see what happens with everything," Christian spoke.

"Yeah, we just have to get you through the next few weeks," Raymond uttered.

Christian displayed a concerned look.

"Everyone has been watching the trial," Raymond started, "and I don't think Charles is really feeling the attention you're getting from the inmates."

"So, you're saying I have to watch out for him?"

"Not just him," Raymond continued. "This whole jailhouse knows that you're here," he shook his head. "While many are hailing you as a hero, there are quite a few that want blood because you put them here. Never get caught lacking," Raymond nudged Christian under the table.

Christian put his right hand discreetly under the table and felt for Raymond's. Christian felt what appeared to be a handle and looked at the item.

"Damn," he spoke disappointedly. "You think it's gotten that deep?" He ran his hand up the shank and stopped once he felt the tip of it.

"Yeah, man," Raymond spoke. "The ones who got you, we got you, but we can't be there all the time."

Christian thought for a minute.

"Nah man, I can't take this. And you can't hold on to it either. We get caught with this thing, that's an automatic few years added," Christian thought about his wife and unborn child. "But I have a plan," he shrugged his shoulders.

As Christian finished speaking, the two were approached by an inmate.

"Christian 'mutha-fucking' Tate," the man spoke as he sat down.

Christian didn't say anything.

"Remember me?" the inmate questioned.

"Jeremy, not today, man," Raymond intervened.

"You busted me on a drug charge," Jeremy continued. "Judge gave me ten years, when all a nigga was doing was doing what he had to do to provide for his family."

Christian was silent.

"I have a year left, so I'm not going to fuck you up," Jeremy laughed. "But just know I'm watching you."

"Look man," Christian responded. "There are quite a few people who want me dead, both here on the inside and out. And if you want me dead, I completely understand. But what would that change?" Christian questioned

Jeremy. "You got one more year; don't blow it, bro. Get out of here and fight to get it expunged from your record," he sympathized.

"How, nigga?!" Jeremy was getting irate. "Ain't no one gonna hire a criminal. I'm going to have to go right back to what I know."

"Here's a little secret," Christian spoke, "you can get nearly anything expunged from your record. Make it like this shit never happened, but you have to keep a level head. You kill me, they will just tack a murder charge and you'll never get out of here," Christian shrugged as he rose to his feet. Raymond stood tall when Christian rose.

Jeremy sternly looked at Christian and then Raymond.

"Got your little posse, huh?" Jeremy scoffed. "Nah, don't worry, cop. You're not even worth it." Jeremy brushed past Christian and Raymond. Christian looked at Raymond before speaking.

"I gotta get the fuck outta here," he shook his head.

11

"They're painting this picture of a perfect schoolboy," Andrew spoke to Christian as they waited for the judge.

"And if that's their goal, mission accomplished," Christian shook his head.

"Well, it's not going too well for them," Andrew whispered. "We've nearly destroyed every witness they've put on the stand."

The judge entered the room and Christian's eyes followed her.

The bailiff brought the courtroom to their feet.

"We're continuing with the prosecutions' witnesses," Tracy spoke as the courtroom sat down.

Christian watched as the jurors murmured amongst each other.

"They're going to put me away," he gasped for air.

Christian observed the eight jurors who were Caucasian and over 50 years of age, staring at him.

He noticed the other four had a confused look on their faces.

"Just keep your head; your time is coming," Andrew whispered as he poured both of them a cup of water.

"Your Honor, we'd like to call Mrs. Theresa Smith to the stand," Judy announced.

Theresa rose to her feet and approached the stand. She looked back at Christian with tears in her eyes. Her piercing blue eyes stared at Christian as though she were screaming: 'I'm going to get you'.

Judy approached once Theresa was sworn in.

"I know this is difficult, so we're going to go slow," Judy spoke softly.

"Thank you," Theresa stated in a low tone.

"How are you doing today, Mrs. Smith?" Judy asked to get Theresa comfortable.

"Well, I'm breathing," she forced a smile.

The jurors sympathized with her and she picked up a Kleenex.

"Every day is a struggle," she continued. "When I wake up in the morning, it seems like I'm living a nightmare when I call out to Benjamin and he doesn't reply to me," she looked around the courtroom. "I go to his room, and his bed is still a mess, the way he left it that day," she chuckled, "his video games and awards are still intact; his controllers are still laid on the bed and haven't been touched," she continued.

"Everything is just the way he left it," Judy gently finished.

Theresa nodded her head.

"Did Benjamin ever have any trouble with the law, Mrs. Smith?"

"Heavens no," she scoffed. "My Benjamin was a good boy. Treated everyone with kindness and was never in any kind of trouble. Whether it be with the police, school officials, classmates — he made friends everywhere he went and got along with everyone."

Andrew chuckled under his breath and pulled a piece of paper from the folder. Judy saw him remove the paper.

"None?" she questioned. Judy wanted to beat Andrew to the question.

"There was one incident," Theresa thought. "He and a student were disagreeing about the Wallace case and a disturbance occurred," she admitted. "So, they suspended him and the young man; Benjamin got two days and the young man got a week."

"So, the other gentleman was the aggressor," Judy suggested.

Theresa nodded her head.

"The principal found that the other student initiated the attack and so he got more time as a result."

Judy looked around the courtroom and paused at the jurors for their reactions.

"How was Benjamin around large crowds?"

"My Benjamin was always the light in a dark room," Theresa bragged. "Everyone loved him, everywhere he went."

Christian watched Theresa's body movements and glanced at Andrew. He looked at what Andrew was scribbling on the notepad and saw a sketch of Theresa.

"What were Benjamin's grades like?" Judy asked.

"Straight 'A' student," she smiled. "He was a bright young man with a bright future," she inhaled sharply. "Too bad his life was cut short by someone he was supposed to be able to trust."

"Objection, Your Honor," Andrew spoke as he looked up from his drawing.

"The jurors will disregard that last statement from the witness," Tracy replied.

The jurors looked at each other.

"Mrs. Smith, was Benjamin a registered gun owner?"

"Yes, he was," Theresa answered. "He took all of his required classes and training in order to be legally licensed to carry."

"And what kind of firearm did your son own?"

Theresa slightly shrugged her shoulders.

"I don't know much about guns," she laughed. "I know it was a handgun." She looked at the jurors. "Due to the increased crime around our area, he obtained it for our protection."

Christian could see that Andrew was giving a lot of thought to what she was saying.

"And do you know where he stored his firearm when it wasn't in use?"

"I'm not too positive of that," Theresa admitted.

"Thank you, Mrs. Smith," Judy walked away and Andrew rose to his feet.

"Mrs. Smith, what do you do for a living?" he started the questioning.

"I work in a restaurant," she spoke. "I wasn't scheduled on that eventful day," she added.

"So, you were at home that day?" he clarified.

"Yes," she answered.

"Mrs. Smith, can you tell us a little more about Benjamin and his academic life?" he changed subjects.

"As I said, my Benjamin was a straight 'A' student; he was in the top 10% of his class," Theresa bragged.

"That's quite the accomplishment," Andrew remarked. "But right now, I want to get a feel of who Benjamin was as an individual. What can you tell me about the altercation that occurred between Benjamin and the other student?"

"What do you want to know?" Theresa asked with a sniffle.

"So many unanswered questions," Andrew started. "Well, for one, what was the reason for the altercation, as told by the principal?"

Theresa inhaled sharply.

"I'm not 100% sure," she hung her head low.

"You're not sure why your perfect son got into an altercation with another student that got him suspended?" Andrew asked.

Theresa searched for an escape.

After roughly fifteen seconds of silence, Andrew continued.

"Is it possible that you're choosing not to remember because of the nature of the altercation? The classmate that your son had an altercation with was Black," Andrew suggested.

"Objection, Your Honor," Judy shouted.

Before Tracy could interject, Andrew continued.

"The principal of the school spoke on the matter and *your son* was suspended from the school because Benjamin taunted the young man about the verdict of the Nanos case," Andrew decided to turn up the pressure.

"Mr. Brownstone," Tracy started.

"He made comments like 'that nigger got what was coming to him', 'he deserved to die', and 'if he complied, he wouldn't be dead today'."

Theresa spoke in between his pauses.

"My boy wouldn't do that," she spoke gently.

"He even went on to make comments about how Nanos did a favor for the country and he went on to quote Tupac: saying 'one less hungry mouth on the welfare'."

Andrew looked Theresa in the eye.

The jurors looked around the courtroom and looks of shock covered their faces.

"Mr. Brownstone, that's enough," Tracy spoke.

"Your son was a damn racist," Andrew slightly nodded his head at Theresa.

"The jury will disregard the last statement from Mr. Brownstone," Tracy spoke sternly and she hit her gavel. "You're treading in hot water, Mr. Brownstone."

Andrew glared at Tracy but quickly composed himself.

"Mrs. Smith, I have a question," he started again. "It is reported that on the night in question that your son had just come from school and was on his way home, but your son had a firearm on him that night."

"Last time I checked, firearms weren't allowed in schools; especially not in high schools," Andrew looked Theresa in her eyes.

Several small gasps were made around the courtroom.

"Maybe he went by the house after school," Theresa suggested.

"But if he happened to go by the house, wouldn't you have seen him?" Andrew tied her up. "You've said it yourself; you didn't have to go on that day."

Theresa was confused.

"Stop playing these mind games with me," she put her hands on her head.

"No games," Andrew spoke. "I'm just feeding you what you fed to the court," he stepped heavily on the floor.

After a few moments of silence, Theresa cleared her throat.

"Benjamin kissed me that morning and told me he was headed to school. I told him to have a good day," she sniffled, "and he walked out the door. I didn't see Benji again until I was called to identify him at the medical examiner's office."

"Mrs. Smith, I feel for you, I really do," Andrew looked at Christian and turned back to Theresa, "but what I'm getting from what you're saying is that Benji had his gun with him, and if that were the case, there's a good chance that he didn't go to school that day," Andrew looked at the jury. Theresa looked at him in awe.

"The reason I'm saying this is because your son and my client ran into each other earlier that day. He was part of numerous protests around the city surrounding the Nanos verdict," he raised his eyebrow at her.

"That's a lie!" Theresa shouted.

Andrew put surveillance images in front of her and pressed a button that displayed the images on the board.

"And I guess these pictures are fabricated as well? Photos of your son wearing the exact same clothing he was wearing when he was shot?"

"Objection, Your Honor," Judy tried to protect her witness. "Badgering the witness."

"Benjamin Smith was seen on surveillance footage. Multiple witnesses and my client saw him at various locations throughout the day," Andrew responded to her objection.

"Overruled," Tracy responded. "But tone it down, Mr. Brownstone," she showed sympathy.

Andrew nodded his head.

"Mrs. Smith, you didn't receive a call from Benjamin's school that day, telling you he wasn't in school?"

"I don't recall a phone call—."

"Because according to the high school's records, Benjamin was marked absent on that day," Andrew adjusted his sports coat.

Theresa was silent.

"So, let me get this straight," he started, "your son was suspended from school due to racist remarks towards an African-American classmate, he owned a .22 caliber handgun, he skipped school on the day in question, was at the scene of many protests, and pulled out his firearm on an upstanding and respected officer of the law?"

Theresa didn't reply.

"Mrs. Smith, I send my condolences to you and your family, but he wasn't the good boy that you want him to be," Andrew spoke softly. "The moment he pulled his weapon on Sergeant Tate, he knew there was no turning back, and knew the repercussions of his actions," Andrew finished.

"Objection, Your Honor!"

"Withdrawn," he walked away. "No further questions, Your Honor," Andrew sat down at the desk.

Theresa was silent.

After a few seconds of silence, Judy spoke again.

"Um," she started, "no further questions, Your Honor."

"You may step down, Mrs. Smith," Tracy responded.

Christian stared at his lawyer in amazement as he took his seat.

For that moment, Christian felt that everything would be alright.

Theresa stepped down from the stand but didn't take her eyes off of Christian.

"You son of a bitch!" she shouted as she ran towards him. "You took my son from me!" she cried as she reached him.

Andrew quickly rose to his feet to defend Christian and the guards ran in.

Theresa hit Andrew with her purse and managed to slap and scratch Christian.

Andrew restrained Theresa and the congregation started shouting.

"Order in my courtroom!" Tracy banged her gavel. "I demand order!"

The guards took hold of Theresa's arms and Andrew looked at her as they held her back.

Tears were in her eyes and she breathed heavily.

Andrew gave a slight smirk and Theresa attempted to attack again. The guards put her in handcuffs and escorted her from the courtroom.

As the guards managed to escort her from the courtroom, the room was filled with multiple loud conversations.

Christian looked at Keisha and saw tears in her eyes and her hands over her mouth.

Tracy banged her gavel three more times.

"Order in this courtroom!" she shouted.

The conversations seemed to cease in an instant.

Andrew looked at the shocked jury and then at Judy; he could see the embarrassment on her face.

This was her witness that could turn this case and flip it to work in her favor.

Although she was hurting and reacted based on the pain, she knew Theresa's image was painted, and if the defense was able to prove what they were saying through their witnesses, she would lose the case.

"The court will take a brief recess to restore order and so that you can clean yourself up, Mr. Tate," she noticed the scratch and blood flowing down his face. "45 minutes," she hit her gavel against the desk.

The courtroom rose to their feet as Tracy entered her chambers.

The jurors exited to the jury room and the officers walked over to Christian.

"Mr. Brownstone, your client will go to the back to clean himself up. As soon as he's finished, we will bring him back to the front," the officer spoke to Andrew.

"Sounds good," Andrew responded.

Andrew patted Christian's shoulder and the officers escorted him into the back.

Andrew pulled his witness list from the folder and skimmed over it.

Moments later, Christian was being escorted back into the courtroom.

Christian sat beside Andrew and the two gave looks of accomplishment to each other.

"Now, we're going to move this case along quickly," Andrew instructed Christian. "That was the last listed witness for the prosecution, so as quickly as we can, we will move along to get you home to your wife and child."

"I want to thank you for all you've done," Christian started to thank Andrew.

"Don't do that," Andrew spoke as he shook his head. "Keep your head in the game. We're close, but we still have to cross the finish line."

Christian nodded his head and the court officer called the court to their feet. The jury re-entered and once they were all in the courtroom, Tracy entered behind them.

The officer sat the courtroom and Tracy finally spoke.

"Call your next witness."

Judy rose to her feet.

"The prosecution rests, Your Honor," she returned to her chair.

"Defense, are we able to proceed with your witnesses, or should we break for the day and pick back up tomorrow?"

"Yes, Your Honor, we are able to continue today," Andrew rose to his feet. "The defense would like to call Anthony Parnell to the stand."

An African-American man in the crowd rose to his feet and adjusted his tie. He walked to the front.

"Ladies and gentlemen, Mr. Parnell is the principal of Rapier Heights," Andrew spoke as Anthony reached the stand and was sworn in.

Andrew walked from behind the desk and approached Anthony.

"Good afternoon, Mr. Parnell."

"Good afternoon," he spoke in a gruff voice.

"I appreciate you taking the time out of your schedule to speak with us today," Andrew started. "I'm not going to take too much time, but if you would, can you please explain your relationship with Benjamin? Were you all close?"

"Benjamin avoided me in any way he could," Anthony chuckled. "He was a smart kid but he had a temper and absolutely no filter."

Andrew stepped backward.

"I think I've interacted with Ben a total of five times while he was enrolled at Rapier Heights."

"Benjamin has been there since freshman year, correct?"

"Yes. He was set to graduate this year," Anthony answered.

Christian looked around and scanned the courtroom.

His eyes stopped on Keisha; tears filled her eyes.

"As I said before, Benjamin was a very bright student. But I didn't get the warmest vibe from him," Anthony looked at the jury. "He rarely looked in my direction, didn't smile at me, and rarely said 'hello'. He was a real character," he scoffed.

"Was he this way with everyone?" Andrew asked.

"Not with his peers," he answered. "Benjamin was a talker and I would see him around the school; very open and conversational, but with me, I didn't get that."

"Mr. Parnell, did you have a conversation with Benjamin regarding the Nanos verdict?"

"Objection, Your Honor," Judy spoke. "Case relevance?"

"Your Honor, the court deserves to know where Benjamin's mental space was regarding surrounding events. everything. This will demonstrate where his head was at the time of the shooting."

"Overruled," Tracy sounded reluctant to speak those words.

"Benjamin and I didn't have a direct conversation regarding the verdict, but I did overhear him talking to his peers; it wasn't anything pretty," Anthony responded as he sat erect in the chair.

"Explain?" Andrew stood beside Christian.

"Just very angry and derogative terminology was used when referencing Wallace. I will say one thing: after the verdict dropped, there was a change in Benjamin's behavior for the worse."

Andrew continued to study the jury and glanced at Tracy.

He knew that Tracy didn't want him to take this route, but the opportunity presented itself, and he couldn't let it pass him up.

"Mr. Parnell, what was the overall genetic makeup of Benjamin's peers?"

"Objection, Your Honor," Judy replied as she wrote notes on her notepad.

"Sustained," Tracy spoke.

"Allow me to rephrase the question," Andrew cleared his throat. "Mr. Parnell, how would you describe the majority of Benjamin's friends?"

"Do you mean their ethnicities?" Anthony asked.

"Yes," Andrew answered.

"Your Honor, I object!" Judy stressed.

"Sustained," Tracy replied. "Mr. Brownstone, I have told you before that we aren't here to make this a case about race. It's about bringing justice regarding the shooting death of Mr. Smith."

Andrew was silent.

"Give me one second, Mr. Parnell," he walked back to the table.

"White," Anthony spoke.

Andrew looked back and paused in his tracks.

"You say something, Mr. Parnell?" Tracy asked.

"The majority were white. The only time I've seen him interact with Black children was when he was trying to intimidate them, have racist remarks, or when he was making them feel inferior." Anthony finished.

"Your Honor, control that witness," Judy interjected.

The jury all let out sounds of shock and awe.

"Do you feel that Benjamin could have been showing this aggressive behavior towards Sergeant Tate on the night of the shooting?" Andrew pushed forward.

"Don't answer that question," Tracy scolded.

Anthony ignored Tracy.

"Benjamin hasn't brought a weapon to school but has exhibited violent behavior towards his African-American peers numerous times. Based on this, in my opinion, Benjamin could have very well exhibited behavior that led to his demise."

"Do you believe that Sergeant Tate shot Benjamin as a result of fear?" Andrew shouted over the crowd.

"Yes, it was fear; nothing but fear. The moment that Benjamin made the adult decision to run from the police and pulled out his weapon, he knew his fate!" Anthony exclaimed over the excitement.

"Get him off the stand," someone in the audience shouted.

The rest of the courtroom erupted with jeers and complaints.

Tracy banged her gavel on the desk.

"People say whatever the hell they want in here," Judy threw her hands in disgust.

"I will have order in this courtroom, or else I will have everyone removed from here!" Tracy shouted.

The courtroom silenced slowly and Tracy continued.

"The jury will disregard the last statements from the witness. Mr. Brownstone," Tracy spoke in a lower tone, "you will *not* continue this behavior."

Andrew nodded his head.

"No further questions, Your Honor," he sat beside Christian.

Judy approached the stand slowly. She studied Anthony for any weaknesses that she could use to exploit him.

"Good afternoon, Mr. Parnell," she spoke.

"Good afternoon," he replied.

"Just a few quick questions," she twitched her neck to pop it. "What was Benjamin's GPA, attendance record, and detention record?"

"Benjamin was one of our brightest students; he had a 3.98 GPA on a 4.0 scale," Anthony spoke eloquently. "He had a pretty solid attendance record up until the Nanos verdict came back, and only a few detentions in his time at Rapier Heights. This was his only behavioral suspension; he had a few in-school suspensions for being tardy, but nothing major."

"Sounds like a remarkable student," Judy suggested.

"He was," Anthony agreed. "I'm not taking that from him."

Andrew saw that Judy wanted to keep the good boy image painted for Benjamin and she was determined to prevent it from being tainted.

"He was a brilliant young man; he could have redirected his energy to positivity though."

"Elaborate," Judy spoke.

Andrew was surprised she didn't stop him from talking.

"As the principal, I saw all of the students around the school and I saw there was a lot of hate in Benjamin's heart. I honestly couldn't tell you why, but he redirected his anger towards African-Americans," Anthony looked at the jury.

The members of the jury showed no emotion and looked blankly.

Judy looked at the jury members and smirked.

"No further questions, Your Honor," she walked away.

***

"*How many interactions did you have with Benjamin?*" Andrew asked the school counselor.

"*I took it upon myself to try to speak to Benjamin quite a bit,*" the counselor answered.

"That your boy's case?" Casey, a fellow inmate, asked Raymond as he watched television.

"Yes, sir," Raymond answered. "It's been a pretty wild day in court, but I think they're doing pretty well."

"*Why is that?*" Andrew asked the counselor.

"*As stated by Mr. Parnell earlier, I could sense there was a lot of hate in Benjamin's heart. From our numerous sessions, I was able to get to the root problem.*"

"*Go on,*" Andrew spoke.

"*Benjamin's racism and hatred was rooted deep and had quite a bit to do with his childhood...*"

Casey pulled out a shank and threw his hand at Raymond's rib cage.

Raymond grabbed Casey's arm and twisted it.

"Shit, shit, shit," he winced with pain as they both rose to their feet.

"Uh-huh," Raymond spoke as he shoved Casey to the ground.

Two other inmates ran over to Raymond with shirts wrapped around their fists.

Raymond put his foot on Casey's back and quickly put his fists up to defend himself from the others.

"Faheem!" the first inmate shouted to one of the newcomers.

Faheem threw a punch at Raymond and he quickly ducked his head to avoid the hit.

Raymond threw two hits and punched Faheem in the face and the rib.

Dayton, the third inmate, ran in and tackled Raymond to the ground.

Casey got off the ground and picked his shank back up.

"You're protecting that nigger," he approached Raymond as he tussled with Dayton on the ground.

Raymond threw his fists into Dayton's back and shoved him to the floor. Raymond quickly jumped to his feet and kicked Dayton and grabbed for Casey.

The alarm to the prison sounded off as Raymond fought the three men. Casey quickly shifted his foot to trip Raymond but as Raymond fell, he pulled Casey to the ground with him.

Faheem hustled over to the two and grabbed the shank from the ground and inserted the blade into Raymond's side.

"Fuck!" Raymond winced with pain before headbutting Casey and knocking him unconscious.

Faheem also slashed at Raymond's leg and the blade connected with his inner thigh.

Although he was in pain, Raymond picked himself up and punched Faheem in the stomach.

Faheem tried to stab Raymond once more, but Raymond caught his fist and redirected Faheem's hand to his neck. He held Faheem's fist in place.

Officers ran into the room with their guns aimed at Raymond.

"Get on the ground!" they shouted.

Raymond was frozen with a mixture of adrenaline and fear of getting shot and killed by the officers.

Blood dripped from his side onto the floor; some landed on Casey's body.

"Drop your weapon!" the officer shouted as he inched closer to Raymond.

Raymond looked at his wounds and released Faheem's fist.

Faheem fell to the ground and Raymond put his hands up and dropped to his knees.

Several officers ran closer and one kicked the shank away.

Charles approached the front and saw the wounds on Raymond.

"Apply pressure to your wound," he spoke with attitude. "Get the medic up here."

Charles scanned the room and saw the other three on the ground. Casey was still unconscious from the headbutt and Faheem was in pain from his wrist being bent backward.
Dayton was in pain due to being hit in the back but laid on the ground with his hands over his head.
"Take these three down to the hole," Charles instructed the officers.
The officers put the three in handcuffs and walked Dayton and Faheem from the room.
Numerous officers carried Casey out.

"Come lay over here," he spoke to Raymond.
Raymond was skeptical at Charles assisting him, but due to his wounds, he laid on the bench.
"The cut seems pretty deep," he glared at Raymond.
"Shit hurts more than it seems," he spoke as the adrenaline died down.
"Guess you got what was coming to you, nigger," Charles uttered as the nurse walked in.

Raymond thought that Charles had come to an understanding as to what Christian would say, considering he was just attacked by three White inmates, but the final statement said everything.

"You a sad nigga," Raymond responded before closing his eyes.

12

Christian entered the prison and noticed how quiet it was. He walked over to the table where Raymond normally sat and saw the police tape blocking the area.
Christian saw a piece of Raymond's bandana on the floor next to a small puddle of blood.
He felt his stomach sink as he feared the worst.
Christian popped his neck and quickly walked to Raymond's cell.
He looked through the bars and saw Raymond sitting on the bench with the gauze over his wounds.
He appeared to be asleep.

"Yo," Christian called to get Raymond's attention.
Raymond opened his eyes and looked at the bars.
"What's up, superstar?" Raymond smirked. "I saw you and your lawyer killing it on TV today."
"Damn all that," Christian retaliated, "what happened to you?"
Raymond chuckled.
"I was approached by some inmates who tried to kill me," he shook his head.
Christian hung his head.

"The fuckas' said I was protecting 'the nigger that killed that gentleman in cold blood'. I knew right then it was going to be something serious," Raymond uttered.

"So, what happened?" he asked softly.

"Well, once the officers finally ran in and broke it up, the three attackers got sent to the hole and Charles' bitch ass stayed with me until the nurse came and wheeled me down to her office," Raymond rolled his eyes. "They patched me up, looked at the security cameras, and saw they were the aggressors before sending me on my merry way. They tried, but the blade missed my rib by about an inch."

A few seconds passed before another word was uttered.

"I'm sorry," Christian replied.

"Why are you sorry?" Raymond laughed. "You have no reason to be sorry because these racist bastards are in here."

"This shit's getting thick," Christian spoke. "And we both have to get out of here before we get killed."

"Like I've told you before," Raymond grunted as he stood and limped towards the bars. "I can hold my own."

"Where was your crew when this shit went down?" Christian thought aloud.

"All around," Raymond spoke. "But none were where I needed them to be," he joked. "I'm going to have to run a tighter ship."

Christian was amazed at how Raymond could chuckle at the situation at hand.

"But tell me about what went down following the counselor. Shit, I was watching him speak when the bastards ran up and attacked me."

"Well," Christian started as he stood at the bars, "once Andrew was done questioning him, that was pretty much the end of that. There wasn't too much that Judy had as a rebuttal."

"I see you all are moving along rather quickly," he expressed.

"Yeah, that's what he told me," Christian started. "Drew told me that once we started our line of questioning, things were going to move quickly."

"I'm going to hold my weight," Raymond held his wound. "But I don't want for you to stress. It's crunch time for you, Boss."

"That's what I'm feeling," Christian agreed. "But we're both going to get out of here, sooner than later. Keep your head and let me know if you need anything, man," Christian spoke as he walked into his cell.

"Bet," Raymond replied before walking back over to the bench.

The next morning, Christian spoke to Andrew before the trial started for the day.

"Someone stabbed him," Christian enunciated. "They got him pretty bad," he shook his head.

"Damn, man," Andrew started. "I'm sorry to hear that happened. How's he holding up?"

"He's tough," Christian spoke. "He's holding his own, but this thing is getting thick," he referred to his case. "These men are out to get me and whoever is helping me."

"Who has your back in the jail besides Ray?"

"It's just Ray and his crew," Christian answered. "I've been trying, but after a certain point, I couldn't keep a low profile," he chuckled. "The case is all over and everyone knows I'm there."

"I know," Andrew spoke. "Well, we're going to try to finish through our witnesses by either today or tomorrow and have you home in no time. Then, I'll devote my energy to getting your boy out."

"Respect," Christian uttered.

The court officer brought the courtroom to a stand as the jury walked in, followed by Tracy.

Once Tracy sat, the courtroom sat, except for Andrew.

"The defense would like to call Lieutenant Samuel Miller to the stand."

Samuel rose to his feet and walked slowly to the witness stand.

Christian didn't take his eyes off of his former supervisor. Part of him was still upset that he didn't defend him as much as he should have, but Christian knew he was also doing his job.

Still, Christian felt he could have done a little more to protect *his* job and integrity. He honestly wasn't too sure about calling him as a witness.

Andrew approached the bench. He was dressed business casual, but not as made up as he normally was.

"Lieutenant Miller, state your business," Andrew instructed.

"Lieutenant Samuel Miller; I'm the head of district 78 and I've been over the unit for the past nine years."

"How long have you been an officer of the law?"

"Going on my 25th year," he spoke clearly.

"That's a long time; thank you for your service to the city," Andrew spoke. Samuel nodded his head.

"Lieutenant Miller, how long have you known my client?"

"I've known Christian Tate for his entire career; ever since he graduated from the academy nine years ago."

"That's a mighty long time," Andrew spoke. "So, you can say that you know my client's ethics and behavior."

"Yes, that's accurate," Samuel replied.

"Lieutenant Miller, can you give a depiction of what happened on the night of March 2nd, 2019?"

Samuel sighed as he remembered what happened.

"On the evening on March 2nd, 2019, at approximately 9:45, Christian Tate answered a call about a suspicious character around 44th and Michigan. He drove to the scene and called out to the man. That's where the pursuit began."

"And how do you know this was the case?" Andrew covered his bases.

"Bodycam footage as well the conversations with Christian Tate and the I.A.D."

"I'm glad you brought that up," Andrew paced back and forth. "But continue with what you know."

"With pleasure," he continued. "Once the pursuit began, I heard Christian Tate announce his presence as Miami P-D numerous times." Samuel nodded to the board. "Once the subject reached the gate, he attempted to climb and although Christian warned him about the potential tasing, he climbed regardless."

Andrew continued to scan the juror's faces for signs of emotion as Samuel gave his testimony.

"Tate walked over to the suspect and a few words were exchanged. The suspect tried to stand on his feet and Tate put his hand on the suspect to sit him down," Samuel was careful with his choice of words.

He didn't want to see Christian go down for doing his job as a police officer.

He already knew how the jury viewed Christian so he knew they would be nitpicking at his word choices.

"As Christian reached for his handcuffs, the suspect leaped to his feet and pulled out a weapon. Once my officer pulled out his weapon, he instructed the suspect to drop his weapon," Samuel looked at the jury and then the judge. "Benjamin thought about his choice and returned his weapon to his waistband and ran. Tate began the chase once more and announced his presence as Miami police." Samuel sighed.

Christian didn't take his eyes off of Samuel; he was wrong about not wanting him to take the stand.

"The subject pulled out his firearm once more and Tate reported that the suspect had a weapon; he instructed him to drop the weapon. The subject lost his footing in the rain and tripped over a root growing from the ground. Christian caught up to him with his weapon aimed. Mr. Smith quickly turned over with his weapon aimed and started to pull the trigger. Tate responded to the movement and fired the deadly shot. He called in the shot to dispatch and requested an ambulance. C.P.R. was performed but to no avail," he finished.

"And you saw all of this on the body camera?" Andrew asked.

"Yes," Samuel replied. "I viewed it shortly after I interviewed Christian. Three hours after the interview with I.A.D."

Andrew improvised; he didn't know that Samuel had seen the full video; the clip they'd received cut off before the shot was fired.

"The clip that I received from the department cuts the video before the shot was fired," Andrew spoke.

"Nope, I saw it as clear as day. I'm not sure why your video cuts out."

"You wouldn't happen to have a copy of the footage, would you?" Andrew asked.

"Afraid not," Samuel answered.

Christian raised his eyebrows as Samuel spoke.

"It's okay," Andrew spoke, trying not to sound defeated. "In your professional opinion, did Christian Tate follow protocol when apprehending the suspect?" Andrew asked.

Judy objected to the question.

"Your Honor, Lieutenant Miller has served the city for over 25 years; I think he's earned the right to speak here today. Plus, the question posed is asking that in all of his years of being an officer, if he feels that the correct protocol was followed."

"Overruled," Tracy adjusted her glasses.

"Yes," Samuel answered. "Sergeant Tate followed all protocols and procedures in apprehending the suspect. There was no foul play or police brutality. No excessive use of force or anything."

Andrew nodded.

"Thank you, Lieutenant Miller," he walked away and sat next to Christian.

"Went better than expected," he whispered to Christian and directed his attention back to the trial.

"It's interesting that you mentioned the body cam footage," Judy spoke.

"Why is that interesting?" Samuel asked.

"The court has seen the body cam footage, and the footage shown by the defense cuts out right before someone falls. Who that someone is, we don't know for certain," she spoke.

"All I can do is report on the video that I saw," Samuel projected.

"Do you have evidence of this video?" Judy asked.

Samuel was silent.

"That's what I thought," she continued. "Lieutenant Miller, have you had any other reports of abuse of power regarding the defendant?"

Samuel gave Judy a look.

"Don't look at me like that," she replied. "There have been numerous reports of comments made by the defendant that haven't been what you would expect from a sergeant of the law."

Samuel and Christian both knew what she was referring to.

"A few weeks before the Wallace verdict, the defendant was overheard making comments like 'I'm tired of my people getting killed and there being no repercussions'. Does that sound like an upstanding officer to you?" Judy asked.

"Objection, Your Honor," Andrew intervened.

"Sustained," Tracy replied.

"Forgive me," Judy replied with a slight smirk. "I'll rephrase," she repositioned herself. "Lieutenant Miller, do you think Christian Tate *was* an officer who included race in the decision-making process for the majority of his cases?"

"Christian Tate was one of the most solid officers in my unit," Samuel started. "Before this incident, he hadn't had to fire his weapon in five years. He always remained levelheaded and used great judgment when solving cases."

Judy looked at Samuel with a serious expression.

"Always?" she questioned.

"*Always,*" Samuel emphasized.

Judy started to walk away and Samuel continued.

"I can not allow for you all to paint this picture of Christian as if he is some kind of criminal," Samuel cleared his throat after speaking.

"That's enough, Lieutenant," Judy spoke. "No further questions, Your Honor."

Samuel glared at her and she smirked back at it.

Andrew approached Samuel once more and gave a slight head nod.

"Lieutenant Miller, Ms. Holloway referenced an incident where Mr. Tate spoke to a coworker about injustices that African-Americans face. You've worked with Mr. Tate for years; can you tell us where you believe his head was at during this time?"

Samuel swallowed air.

"Sergeant Tate has been in my unit for seven years; he's typically the first one in and the last officer to leave for the evening. He's the one to thank for the city being so clean," Samuel chuckled. "I mean, I could take credit, but Sergeant Tate has been a blessing to this city, especially in areas where I was lacking and wasn't quite as efficient. When this was brought to my attention, I immediately thought of the verdict and all of the cases that could have made him make such a statement."

Samuel paused and looked at the jurors.

"Trayvon Martin, Eric Garner, Sandra Bland, Sam Dubose, Philando Castile, Oscar Grant, Alton Sterling, just to name a few... So, I can understand his comments, to be honest," Samuel spoke, "but I know the way he felt about the unjust treatment and killings had absolutely nothing to do with *this* shooting."

"Thank you, Lieutenant Miller," Andrew walked to the desk and shuffled his papers in the folder. A few seconds later, he looked up at Tracy.

"No further questions, Your Honor."

"You may step down, Lieutenant Miller," Tracy remarked.

Samuel rose from the stand and stepped down.

"Your Honor, for the final witness, the defense would like to call Christian Tate to the stand," Andrew projected.

There were several hushed murmurs around the courtroom.

Tracy lightly tapped her gavel on the desk.

"Court officer, escort Mr. Tate to the stand."

This was it; the moment that Andrew and Raymond had both been speaking about and Christian knew it.

The court officer slowly approached Christian as his thoughts raced.

He knew he had this one opportunity to leave an impression on this jury or else, they would send a verdict of 'guilty' and lock him away for years; all for doing his job.

His life was in the hands of a majority-white female jury.

Christian walked with the court officer to the stand and he sat down. He was sworn in and Andrew approached him.

"Hello, Mr. Tate," Andrew spoke sternly.

"Good afternoon," Christian spoke. Even though fear filled his body, he didn't let it show.

"Mr. Tate, how long have you had your rank of 'Sergeant' here in the city of Miami?"

"I have been the sergeant of my unit for roughly six years," he spoke clearly into the microphone.

"And in the six years, have you ever received any violations or complaints of police misconduct?" Andrew didn't waste any time.

"I haven't received any violations," Christian replied. "In all honesty, this is my first offense."

"We've heard the story numerous times," Andrew spoke, "but would you mind walking us through what happened on that fateful night?"

Christian sighed and nodded his head.

"I live this day over and over; when I'm in my cell, at lunch, working out; it doesn't matter. March 2nd, 2019, 9:00: I got a call from Officer Daniel Rogers; he wasn't coming in and was taking a sick day," Christian recalled all of the events the evening. "Although I don't normally patrol, I went out to cover for my coworker. While patrolling, I got a call over the radio about a suspicious character around 44th and Michigan."

Christian made sure to make eye contact with the jurors while speaking.

"Since I was already in the area, I responded to the call and announced I would be checking it out. When I got to the area, I noticed it was only illuminated by one street light and my vehicle's headlights, so I used my spotlight and shined it over by the bushes."

Christian glanced over at Judy, who was anxiously looking through her notes for cross-examination.

He continued to tell his story.

"Once the spotlight was on the bushes, I saw the man crouching down as if he were hiding."

"I'm assuming the man you're referring to is Benjamin," Andrew suggested.

"Correct," Christian spoke. "I exited my vehicle and called over to Benjamin," he cleared his throat. "This is when he began to run. I chased him and told him to stop running or that he would be tased. He tried to climb the gate and I fired the taser. His scream: it was a piercing scream and I hear it every day."

Christian wasn't necessarily trying to gain sympathy from the jurors, but he was telling the truth. Since the shooting, he felt haunted.

"Benjamin fell to the ground and as I got closer, I noticed that I'd seen Benjamin earlier that day."

"Where did you encounter Benjamin?" Andrew asked.

"Earlier in the day, when myself and my partner, Officer Francesca Gaines, went by the supermarket and I saw Benjamin. He was wearing a MAGA hat and he gave me a specific look."

"What kind of look?" Andrew questioned.

"Objection, Your Honor. We have no way of verifying the 'looks' that were exchanged between the defendant and the deceased."

"Sustained," Tracy responded.

"Proceed with your story," Andrew nodded for Christian to continue.

Christian nodded his head.

"I asked Benjamin why he was running to which he replied 'f you' and tried to raise to his feet. I put my hand on his shoulder and applied a small amount of force to sit him back down."

The jurors stared at Christian and he could feel the spotlight was on him but he didn't let the pressure phase him.

"When I reached behind me to pull out my handcuffs, Benjamin jumped to his feet, reached behind him, and pulled out a weapon."

"Is this weapon the same handgun that's entered as exhibit 73.4 C?" Andrew questioned.

"Yes," Christian answered. "The .22 caliber handgun; I was a little shocked at how quickly everything escalated."

"What was going through your mind at that moment?" Andrew asked.
"Everything went blank once I saw the weapon aimed at me. My wife was on my mind, Benjamin was in my thoughts as I wondered what he could have had on him to cause him to draw the weapon. I had no choice but to draw my weapon and aim. I shouted for Benjamin to drop the weapon. I guess when he saw my weapon was out and heard my order, he figured it would be easier to run from me. He returned his weapon to his waistband and began running again. I reported that he began fleeing once more and I chased behind him."
"But wasn't he just tased? Doesn't that normally have an effect on a suspect?"
"Normally, yes. I'm not sure what was the case with Benjamin, but it seems as though the electricity did not affect him," Christian answered.

The looks on the jurors' faces didn't change; it looked to Andrew as if they'd already made up their mind and decided Christian's fate.

"I announced my presence as Miami P.D. once more and I saw Benjamin slide his hand into his waistband. I reported that he had a weapon. It was raining and Benjamin tripped over a root that was growing from the ground and fell on his stomach. I was able to catch up with him."
Christian inhaled sharply.
"I approached with my weapon aimed since I saw he was fidgeting with his while he was running. I told him not to move and to remain on his stomach with his hands extended. Benjamin quickly flipped over with his weapon aimed and loaded. He started to pull the trigger and I responded to the slight movement; I fired my weapon and the bullet struck Benjamin in the chest. He fell back to the ground and I approached with my weapon aimed. I kicked his firearm away from his body and kneeled. I performed chest compressions, but no luck."
"I'm sorry this happened," Andrew spoke once Christian finished. "This experience has to be a terrifying one."
"It is," Christian replied.
Andrew walked away and Judy approached Christian.

"Mr. Tate, I'm having a little trouble piecing a few things together," she held a notepad full of notes, "perhaps you can assist me."

Christian glared at Julie.

"When Benjamin was shot, how did his body return to the earth? We have images of him lying on the ground as if he were shot while fleeing from you."

"When Benjamin was about to fire his weapon, I shot him in the chest and I guess the power from the shot literally flipped him around. I don't have to lie about that," Christian didn't get upset.

He'd worked with Judy on numerous cases and she knew he wouldn't do anything to jeopardize his job, but at that moment, he was the enemy and she still had a job to do as the prosecutor for the case.

"How often is it that a shot turns someone's body around?" Judy challenged Christian.

"Is that a rhetorical question?" Christian asked. "Ms. Holloway, you've worked with my former unit for years, so there's no need for you to act as if you don't know that that happens," he replied.

Andrew shook his head at Christian.

The jury detected Christian's attitude and several women rolled their eyes.

"Mr. Tate, in your initial statement to Lieutenant Miller, you said, and I quote, 'I instructed the gentleman once more to drop his weapon'," Judy alternated her eye contact between the jurors and Christian. "'He didn't listen and adjusted his finger on the trigger. I had a choice to make and I made it.' End quote," she finished. "What did you mean by that?"

Christian wasn't sure if he should answer the question or not.

He looked at Andrew and then at Samuel.

Samuel had a stern expression on his face and held his head high as he sat erect in the crowd.

There were no objections made by Andrew and Judy spoke again.

"You don't have an answer to that question?"

"Any answer that I give you will be taken out of context," Christian replied. "You have a job to do, I understand, but the fact that you're asking me that question tells me that you're trying to flip my words around."

"So, no direct answer as to what you meant?" Judy insisted.

Christian glared at her.

"Me saying that 'I had a choice to make and I made it' implied that I did what I was trained to do in order to disorient the suspect. However," Christian adjusted himself in the seat, "what you failed to mention was that I told my superior officer that I performed chest compressions after the shot was fired. I administered C.P.R. to Benajmin, but to no avail. This *was* demonstrated in the case, but I guess you're choosing to gloss over it," he suggested.

Judy was embarrassed but she didn't let Christian or the court see it.

"Oh, you mean the C.P.R. that did more harm than good?" Judy smirked.

"Objection, Your Honor," Andrew uttered.

"Withdrawn," she remarked. "No further questions," Judy walked away and back to her desk.

Andrew rose to his feet and walked back over to Christian.

"Really quickly, Mr. Tate," he asked with a serious tone to his voice, "do you feel you followed the protocol when apprehending Mr. Smith?"

"Yes," Christian answered.

Andrew nodded his head slightly and slowly paced the floor. He walked towards the jury box.

"Mr. Tate, do you regret the decisions that you chose to take that night; starting from accepting the call?"

Christian thought about his answer to this question as the entire courtroom fell silent.

All eyes were on him as this question was posed and Christian knew it. He looked around the courtroom as the jurors waited in anticipation for his answer.

Christian looked down at his hands and looked back up. He made eye contact with Keisha and she mouthed out 'I love you'.

Christian inhaled and sighed before answering.

Back at the jailhouse, numerous inmates were watching the trial; some that were on Christian's side and others who felt that Christian was in the wrong.

"Come on, man," Raymond spoke under his breath.

"No," Christian finally answered, "I don't regret any of the decisions that I made on that evening," Andrew started to walk away from him.

There were several murmurs around the courtroom and in the jailhouse; Christian even heard Tracy gasp softly.

Christian knew that everyone around America was now talking about the case and his reply, but he didn't care.

He spoke his truth, and that was all he knew. He knew that it was either him or Benjamin.

Christian didn't shoot to kill Benjamin; if that were the case, he wouldn't have even attempted C.P.R. He just needed to make sure everyone else understood that.

"No further questions, Your Honor," Andrew announced as he got back to the table.

Christian looked at the jurors and saw the expressions on their faces; they were all but pleasant.

The court officers approached the bench and Christian rose to his feet.

The officers escorted Christian over to the desk and Andrew nodded to him.

"Are there any further witnesses from either party?" Tracy asked.

"The Prosecution rests, Your Honor," Judy spoke.

"The Defense rests, Your Honor," Andrew announced.

Tracy looked at the clock on the wall and figured it would be a good time to dismiss court for the day.

"Let's break for the day," Tracy spoke. "Tomorrow at 9, we will resume the trial with closing statements."

Tracy hit her gavel on the stand and Christian sternly looked at Andrew.

"We got this," he remarked.

***

13

Judy collected all of her notes and approached the front.

"At the beginning of the case, during the opening statement, we said that this was a case of murder. What has the evidence that we have brought before you proven?" she started. "It was roughly 80 degrees and raining on the night of March 2nd, 2019, and Benjamin Smith was walking home," Judy continued.

She had to find ways to change her statement since multiple holes were poked in her defense.
"Here are some of the facts: We know that Benjamin was on his way home that evening. We know that Benjamin decided to stray away from his normal route to get home to stop at the convenience store. We know that he was on the ground when the deadly shot was fired and we also know that he had tripped before he was shot, which leads us to the understanding that he was defenseless at the time," Judy sipped her water. "In short, we have shown, and the defense concedes, that Christian Tate shot and killed Benjamin Smith; the only remaining question is whether that killing is a murder. The evidence that we have presented during the course of this trial clearly establishes that the defendant is guilty of first-degree murder, aggravated battery, and official misconduct."

Christian shook his head slightly as Judy spoke, but he didn't show his frustration.

"How did Benjamin get to the point of being shot while on the ground by law enforcement? Let's walk through it," Judy recited.

Christian could tell this was a speech that she'd practiced as she looked directly at the jury while speaking.

"Benjamin Smith was headed home from being a teenager. Should he have been in school that day? Absolutely," Judy addressed the report that he was absent from school that day. "However, what teenager do you know that doesn't skip school? You've done it, I know I've done it, and I know you know a child who's done it."

The jury members each looked at each other.

"Benjamin was walking home from a long day of teenaging down Michigan. But before completing his journey home, he stopped at a convenience store," Judy knew she was on thin ice by bringing up the convenience store, but she had a case to win. "He went into the store with the hopes of buying the normal junk food a teenager loves to consume; candy, chips, and a Brisk iced tea with lemon," she showed the images of the items that were recovered from Benjamin's body at the scene.

"Benjamin and the clerk exchanged a few choice words, as you fine men and women saw earlier, and Benjamin exited the store with his items. He paid for the items with cash before leaving. He spent all of five minutes in the store before continuing his walk home," Judy switched images on the screen to show the still image from the security camera of Benjamin leaving the store. "Not even two minutes after leaving the store, he was confronted by Christian Tate. A straight-A student fled, as he was unaware that Christian Tate was law enforcement. Did the defendant announce his presence as law enforcement, yes, but there had been so many African-American men modifying their vehicles so that they could pass as law enforcement around the time of the shooting."

Christian shook his head at what she was saying.

"Should Benjamin have run? No. Was he in the wrong in that sense?" she scanned the jury. "Absolutley," she answered her question. "As Benjamin ran to create space between himself and the defendant, the defendant pulled out his taser and electrocuted Benjamin. This shock sent 1200 volts of electricity through Benjamin's 140-pound body. The defendant wasn't aware if Benjamin had medical issues; if he had a mental illness; he didn't *know* my client. Not to mention," she cleared her throat, "when Benjamin was tased, he was climbing a fence and was at least ten feet off the ground, so as the electricity ran through his body, he fell on his back, back down to the Earth."

Judy did her best to use her closing remarks to paint Benjamin out to be a victim.
Andrew took notes on what Judy was saying. He knew he'd have to modify his closing argument to counter hers. However, he wanted to ensure his counter closing argument was solid enough so that she wouldn't have much of a rebuttal.

"140 pounds falling to the Earth from sixteen feet in the air in under 1 second," Judy emphasized. "Imagine the pain that had to go through Benjamin's body."
She saw some of the female jurors accumulate tears in their eyes. Judy felt accomplished by seeing this.

"The defendant approached Benjamin and pushed him down as he tried to sit up and Christian pulled out his handcuffs. A straight 'A' student who'd never been in trouble with the law; he was scared, so he pulled out his firearm and aimed it, out of fear," Judy was careful with her words. "When the defendant instructed Benjamin to put his weapon away, he obeyed, but he fled once more. It was a mixture of fear and adrenaline that allowed him to run, regardless of the fact that 1200 volts of electricity had just shocked his heart. This is when the video of the body camera goes dark and all we hear is audio."

Judy pressed a button on the remote she was holding and the slideshow switched to the next slide. She walked over to the board and pressed the spacebar on the keyboard attached and the video started to play.

"*Miami P-D, drop your weapon,*" they heard Christian shout but saw a dark screen.
Judy was silent while the video played.
There was the sound of Benjamin tripping and falling; footsteps could be heard quickly approaching him.
"*Stay on your stomach with your hands extended!*"
No further words were spoken and there was no video, but the sound of the footsteps ceased and a few seconds later, the gunshot erupted; many of the jurors jumped at this.
Judy stopped the video and continued.

"That's the end of the video," she paused for effect. "It ends with a gunshot, which you have heard from the defendant himself, that he fired the shot. You heard from the ballistics expert that the bullet retrieved from the crime scene matches the police-issued handgun that was assigned to Mr. Tate."
Judy clasped her hands together.
"You heard from the city's pathologist as well as the private pathologist; both of whom confirmed that the bullet that killed 18-year-old Benjamin Smith was from the defendant's weapon. The private pathologist even went a step further and testified that the C.P.R. administered by the defendant aided in Benjamin's loss of life," she spoke passionately before walking back to her desk and taking a sip of water.
She returned the glass to the tabletop and walked back towards the jury.

"By now, you all are probably asking why this shooting happened and if there was a motive behind it," she asked after clearing her throat. "As logged, Christian has told his previous coworkers that he, and I quote, hoped there was justice for Sterling Wallace because he was tired of them killing us and there being no repercussions for it, end quote. 'Them' being White police officers and 'us' being Black people," she spoke clearly.

"Nanos was found not guilty by the jury, and so Christian Tate decided to take the law into his own hands and ensure there was justice served."

Christian nudged Andrew under the table to get his attention.
Andrew touched Christian on the shoulder and tapped on the notepad. Christian wrote on the pad, 'you're going to let her tear me down like this?'. Andrew read his question and motioned for Christian to take it easy, as though to imply that he was plotting a good reply to her.

"Please keep in mind, however, that we are not required to prove a motive for the shooting. The Court will instruct you on this point later. All we are required to prove, and we have proved, is that the defendant shot and killed Benjamin Smith, he intended to do it, and was not justified in doing so," she cleared up her earlier comment. "It's just that based on his previous comments and actions, it's the logical argument."

Judy walked closer to Tracy but continued to look at the jurors.

"What would the defense have you believe?" she started again. "The defendant states that he was working late and was covering for his coworker who couldn't show up that day. He claims he received a call about a suspicious character and went to the area to investigate. He states that once he saw Benjamin, that's where everything began. The chasing, the tasing, and the fatal shot. And," she added, "we know that he knew it was Benjamin because Christian told us himself that he ran into Benjamin earlier that day."
Judy walked closer to the jury box once again.
"We have, then, a classic case of testimony that as far as what happened on March 2nd is concerned, is contradictory, and it's your duty to decide where the truth lies. In other words, you've got to decide which witnesses are telling the truth. When you decide on the credibility of the witnesses, the court will tell you that you should consider their demeanor while testifying, gauge it against other testimony, measure it against your common sense and experiences in life, and see if the witnesses have any bias, interest, or motive that could affect their testimony."

Christian turned slightly and faced Keisha. She blew him a kiss and put her hand on her belly bump.

His heart fluttered and he smiled at the thought of Keisha bearing his seed, but he remembered there was a chance he wouldn't be able to be there with his family.

Christian turned around and faced the front of the courtroom.

"All of the witnesses that were called have been able to argue that Benjamin was an upstanding citizen. Did he have his set of issues? Of course," Judy answered, "but what person doesn't? It has been testified that Benjamin's adrenaline was high at the time of his death," Judy paced.

Christian cleared his throat.

"The defendant and the video both prove that there was a chase that ensued. As an officer of the law, a sergeant at that, Benjamin should have *not* been tased after running at full speed and leaping on a fence to climb."

Christian raised his eyebrows at what she was saying.

"Once he was shot, with his adrenaline being high, his heart was already racing. Christian Tate knew this from his experience as an officer of the law, so for him to say that he felt the C.P.R. would help, is utter nonsense," she continued.

Andrew continued to jot down notes as Judy spoke. He could tell Christian was getting upset, but he gave a slight motion to him.

"You even had Anthony Parnell address the fact that Benjamin was a tremendous student but he testified that Benjamin's anger and racism stemmed from his childhood," she shook her head slightly. "We all know mental illness is real and exists, and it often stems from the past," she provided reasoning for Benjamin's comments towards the clerk. "If Byron Gates, the school counselor, testifies that Benjamin wasn't fully healthy inside, that should tell you that something could have been going on at the time of the shooting."

The jurors each looked at one another; the majority of them had approving looks.

"Police officers are allowed to carry deadly weapons; they have hands on training for these weapons. Officers can use deadly force *only* when it's necessary," Judy glanced at Christian. "An officer can order you to stop and tell you to follow their orders; they can even arrest you under certain circumstances. However, they can not use deadly force in situations where it doesn't deem fit," she took a dramatic pause. "Ladies and gentlemen, this wasn't a just shooting," she slightly shook her head.

"A person commits the crime of murder when he, first, performs an act or acts which cause the death of another; second, intended to kill or do great bodily harm to another; and third, was not justified in killing the other person under the circumstances," Judy prepared to end her statement. "We have demonstrated, with convincing, credible, and consistent witnesses, that the defendant, Christian Tate, killed the victim, Benjamin Smith, and that he did so intentionally, and that by no stretch of the imagination was this a legitimate situation in which he feared for his life. Each of the witnesses demonstrated that Benjamin was a young man with a promising future. Benjamin came into contact with the defendant and fled out of fear. He had never been in trouble with the law and so he didn't know how to respond. Knowing what you know, we ask that you return the only verdict that this evidence supports and fairness demands, a verdict finding the defendant, Christian Tate, guilty of the crime of first-degree murder, the counts of official misconduct, and aggravated battery. Thank you," Judy returned to her chair and studied the jurors' expressions.

She had a feeling of accomplishment and as a result, she smiled slightly.

Andrew looked at Christian and nodded his head. He slowly rose to his feet before glancing at the clock.
Andrew slowly approached the jurors and Christian watched his every movement.

"Ladies and gentlemen, at the beginning of this case, when her Honor was questioning you, she asked whether you would follow the law, whether you would be fair, and whether you would hold the prosecutors to their burden of proving Christian Tate guilty beyond a reasonable doubt. There was a lot of talk about that and each of you indicated and promised that you would hold the prosecutors to their burden. The judge also asked you whether you would presume Christian innocent throughout this entire trial and through your deliberations, and presume him so unless the State was able to prove him guilty beyond a reasonable doubt. All of you indicated that you presumed him innocent. Additionally, ladies and gentlemen, you were asked to use your common sense and experiences in life in evaluating the testimony of the witnesses. Based upon your responses, you were selected as jurors in this case. We are calling upon you now to abide by the promises you made," Andrew spoke.

The jury stared at Andrew blankly. He didn't pay the looks any attention. "Let's take a look at the evidence and see why the prosecutors have failed to prove Christian Tate guilty beyond a reasonable doubt. As we told you at the beginning, this was a justified shooting, as Christian feared for his life. We do not contest the fact that Benjamin Smith was shot and killed, an unfortunate thing that happened, and nothing that I can say, nothing that anyone in this courtroom can do will change that," Andrew made eye contact with Benjamin's parents before continuing. "The question here is: was Christian Tate *justified* in defending himself under the circumstances that existed that night?"
The jurors looked from Andrew to Christian, and back to Andrew.
"Our answer, ladies and gentlemen, is that the evidence indeed shows that the State failed to prove Christian Tate guilty beyond a reasonable doubt because they did not prove that when he shot Benjamin Smith, he did not *reasonably* believe that it was a necessity to defend himself against death or great bodily harm," he inhaled sharply.

"Now why do I say this? Ladies and gentlemen, basically it comes down to what you believe," Andrew slowly paced the floor as he spoke. "Do you believe what was testified by William Longon, Patricia Young, or Theresa Smith on that stand, or do you believe the defendant, Anthony Parnell, and

Lieutenant Samuel Miller? We have diametrically opposed versions in this case as to what happened."

Christian looked at Tracy to see if there was anything he could gather from her mannerisms; there was nothing.

"The witnesses called by the prosecution have each and all been desecrated in terms of credibility; they each seem to have an underlying motive," Andrew continued and looked at his notepad. Let's take Mr. Oliver Warren, the private pathologist. You remember when he testified to the number of autopsies performed by his office? He reported that 200 out of 1500 autopsies were done on 'my people', I mean people of color," Andrew threw in the remark. "However, his own practice's website reports that only fifty autopsies were performed on African-Americans," Andrew looked at the jurors.

They gave inquisitive looks.

"Which one is the truth? It's hard to decipher." Andrew shifted his body slightly. "What about Patricia Young?" he asked. "Ms. Young was Mr. Smith's best friend; she paints the image of Benjamin to be a happy, smiling, young man who treated everyone with dignity and respect; yet, we have reports that he was rude to a good number of his African-American peers, and there's a video of him speaking pugnaciously to the convenience store clerk just moments before his contact with Christian Tate. Or, how about we switch to Mr. William Longon, who mentioned nothing about Benjamin's mental health, but the assistant principal, Anthony Parnell, who only met with Benjamin on a few occasions, spoke on it?" Andrew raised his tone. "Let's not even touch on the fact that Benjamin attended a predominantly Caucasian school and was taking a course titled 'Negroes in Law Enforcement'," he shook his head.

The courtroom was silent as Andrew spoke and it was apparent they were giving meticulous thought to what he was saying.

Andrew cleared his throat and continued.

"Let me break this down for you and I would like for you all to picture what I am telling you," Andrew began to tell a story. "Imagine being a teenager; you're a straight-A student, popular with the ladies, everything is going perfect. You have a bright future, but your upbringing has scarred you and embedded you with hate," Andrew made references to what was testified by Anthony and demonstrated by Theresa. "You skip school and carry your handgun to show it off to your friends, thinking it makes you 'fresh' and 'lit'. You go to these peaceful protests with a firearm in your waistband with the intention of using it if need be, but nothing occurs, so you can't show your friends how cool you are," Andrew looked at the jury and Christian continued to sit tall.

"So, later, you go to the store to purchase a few snacks for the evening: hot chips, Brisk Iced Tea, and Nerds. Benjamin had what they would call the munchies and the only reason I say that is because marijuana was found in Benjamin's system as well as on his person, as testified by the medical examiner."

Judy sipped on her water and took notes on her notepad for her potential rebuttal.

"After you shout a few demeaning words to the store clerk, you then leave the store with your belongings in your pockets. A short time later, you talk to your best friend on the phone and, you know how it was back in the day when you would do random things while having a good conversation?" he rhetorically asked the jury. "This is one of those times; you decide to crouch between bushes. Benjamin wasn't searching for anything," he rolled his eyes, "nothing was ever recovered from the area," he referenced Patricia's testimony. "You see a police car approach with his lights and siren on. Now," he briefly paused, "let's assume you believe the officer to be an impersonator, so you run. He announces his presence as Miami P-D, but you continue running. You hear him making calls on the radio and he threatens to tase you if you don't stop running. You ignore the threat, and continue running until you reach a fence. You try to climb the fence and jump over when you feel a jolt of electricity flow through your body. You fall to the Earth and you see the man approaching you. You see his badge and hear transmissions coming through his radio, and you try to rise to your feet. His hand gently pushes you down to the ground, and you see him pull out his handcuffs."

Christian opened his eyes widely and looked at the jurors. Some of them had astonished looks on their faces.

"Remembering you had the marijuana on you and in your system, you leap to your feet out of fear and pull out your weapon. You aim it at the man you have now identified as law enforcement and you watch him quickly draw his weapon. He instructs you to drop your weapon. You've never been in any trouble with the law, so you obey his command and lower the item. You return it to your waistband, rather than dropping it, but instead of surrendering, you flee again."

Christian could see the jurors were paying attention to his story to try to find the flaws. He looked at Keisha and she gave him an approving nod.

"You're running so quickly and are so determined to get away, that you begin reaching for your weapon. And in the process of doing so," he projected in such a sense that Christian got chills, "you trip and fall over a root that you didn't notice protruding from the ground. As you're lying flat on your stomach, you hear footsteps approaching. In an attempt to protect your rep and cool points, you aim the weapon once more. The officer quickly pulls out his weapon and instructs you to drop the weapon once more. As you begin to pull the trigger, the officer beats you to it. And fires a single shot," he spoke and seemed to enunciate each word.

The jurors were silent and gave concerning looks as a few of them took notes.

"The force of the blast is so great that it flips you around and causes you to lay on your stomach as you bleed. You hear the words, 'shots fired by the police' and feel the officer turn you over and begin to do chest compressions. You feel the chest compressions as he desperately tries to keep you on this earth and you smirk. Your final words on this Earth are to the officer trying to save your life are chilling."

Andrew knew he was about to drop a bombshell on the jurors that he knew would leave them speechless, so he took his time with expressing it.

"With your dying breath, you manage to emit a chuckle and utter the words: 'still'," he took pauses in between the final words, "'a – nigga'."

The jurors were all shocked and it showed.

14

Christian sat in the weight room with Raymond as he awaited his fate. The closing arguments were finished and now it was up to the jurors to decide what would occur.

Would they see him as an enforcer or as a criminal who had nothing but hatred and vengeance in his eyes and heart?

"Come on, keep your head up," Raymond encouraged as Christian spotted him. "You've got this case in the bag."
"Yeah, but what if the jury comes back with the guilty verdict?" Christian asked. "Bro, I can't do life in prison and I definitely couldn't survive knowing she could give me capital punishment. I couldn't even be there for the birth of my son because of this shit."

Raymond shook his head as he lifted.
"It's fucked up, I'll give you that. It's sad that you were at the very top of things; you have to pull your weapon one time and they strip all of your rights, throw you in jail, and put your fate in the hands of this white... wait, are they white? You know we don't see them on TV" he chuckled.
"Yes."

"Yeah, so they throw your fate into the hands of these white jurors with a white judge. Meanwhile, you got cats like Zimmerman and Nanos walking around freely."

Christian slightly shrugged his shoulders as he listened to the television as he spotted Raymond.

"And the jurors are now entering their second week of deliberations in the highly profiled State of Florida versus Tate case, in which an 18-year-old male was shot and killed by Sergeant Christian Tate. Tate has since been arrested and charged with first-degree murder, two counts of aggravated battery, and three counts of official misconduct."

Christian's heart started to beat quickly as he listened to the reporter. Raymond set the bar on the stands and sat up. He put his hand on Christian's shoulder.

"If found guilty of first-degree murder, Tate could be issued the death penalty, in which case, he would be moved from the facility he's in, to a different one across the city. If found not guilty on the first-degree murder charge but guilty on the others, he could be sentenced up to 25 years behind bars."

Raymond picked the remote off the stand and changed the channels.

"Don't even worry about that," Raymond spoke. "You got one of the best lawyers around; trust me, I watched the case."

As Raymond finished speaking, Charles entered the room.

He slowly approached Christian and Raymond before taking off his sunglasses.

He sucked his teeth before speaking.

"You have some visitors," he spoke to Christian.

"Who is it?" Christian asked.

"Get ya' ass up and see," Charles spoke with aggression.

Christian shook his head and fist-bumped with Raymond.

"I'll be back, dog," he spoke. "Be easy."

"Man, I'm just tryna be like you," Raymond joked as Christian walked away with Charles.

"Man, you sissies are getting out of line with questioning my authority," Charles spoke. "You think the trial is over so you can backtalk now, huh?"

Christian ignored the confrontation attempt.

Charles escorted Christian to the interview room and Christian saw Andrew and Judy sitting in the room.
Charles left the room and Christian sat beside his lawyer.
"What's going on?" he questioned.
"I'm not going to lie to you," Judy began. "The fact that the jury is taking so long to come back means that they are giving some serious thought to this case," she cleared her throat. "They could come back with a guilty verdict and it would be a shame for that to happen," she implied.

Christian raised his eyebrows.
"They'll see and rule on the truth," Christian spoke.
"Let's hear what she has to say," Andrew suggested.
"Here's what I propose," she opened her folder and laid out various pieces of paper. "You plead guilty, and I'll knock the charge down to involuntary manslaughter and one count of official misconduct. I'll drop the aggravated battery charges," she nodded her head slowly. "You'll lose your license and job, but you'll be out in five," she finished.
"No deal," Christian immediately replied. "I'm not pleading guilty to something I'm not guilty of," he shook his head.
Andrew agreed.
"My client was doing his job at the time of the shooting. I know you have a quota to meet," Andrew spoke sternly, "and your success rate is on the line, but you can't possibly think he would accept the deal."
"It's something to think about," Judy continued. "If found guilty, you're looking at the death penalty, Christian," she explained.
"And if found not guilty, I walk," he added. "I'd much rather take my chances than to admit guilt to something that I didn't do."

Judy looked at Andrew.
"You don't want to talk to your client?" she asked.

"The decision's already been made," Andrew suggested, "and it's not changing."

"You might want to think about it before the jury decides to come back," she hinted. "This offer is only good while we're in this room right now," Judy moved her hair from her face. "You face the first-degree murder charges, you won't ever get a chance to see your wife and child from beyond prison windows, *ever.*"

Christian felt a chill run down his spine as she spoke.
He shivered at the fear of not being able to touch Keisha ever again and not being able to hold his son. But he couldn't bring himself to pleading guilty to something he didn't do.

"Plead guilty and the five-year deal is yours. Involuntary manslaughter and one count of official misconduct."
"You know what's interesting," Christian replied.
Andrew and Judy both looked at him.
"No, I don't want to spend my life in jail," he shook his head, "hell, I would take the 5 years, but honestly, I don't want to spend one more night in this hellhole. But, I know you, Judy," he continued.
Judy raised an eyebrow at Christian.
"Yeah, the jury is taking a long while to come back, but they could also come back with a verdict of 'not guilty', and if they do, it will impact your prosecution record. That's the only reason you're here trying to cop a deal."
Andrew smirked at her as Christian finished.
"Don't try to play one of your own," Christian spoke. "You know damn well that I was a great cop and followed everything to the tee," he spoke to her the way he normally would. "You know I followed protocol that night, as I have throughout my entire tenure. Not once have I ever been written up or verbally informed about misconduct."

Judy didn't reply. She pointed to the paper before speaking.
"The deal is *only* valid for the next five minutes."
"No," Christian spoke as he slid the paper away from him.
Judy looked at Andrew sternly.

Andrew slightly shrugged his shoulders.

"It's his decision. I can't force him to take the deal if he feels it isn't a good one. Plus," Andrew pointed out, "he's a cop. He knows the law better than anyone."

"He *was* a cop," Judy corrected as she rose to her feet and returned the paper to the folder.

Judy tapped on the window and Charles opened the door.

"Foolish choice," she replied.

"Thanks for coming," Christian smirked.

Charles closed the door behind Judy and Christian continued to speak to Andrew.

"Do you think that was a smart thing to do?" he asked.

"She's worried," Christian explained. "The case could swing either way and she knows it. Especially because this jury is taking forever to come back with a verdict."

Andrew nodded with an understanding.

"Have you done any more digging about the bodycam footage?" Christian switched subjects.

"No luck as of yet," Andrew answered. "I'm hoping to have it resolved before the jury comes back."

"That could be by tomorrow," Christian shrugged his shoulders.

"Exactly," Andrew added. "We're going to figure this out."

■■

"I understand that you all have reached a verdict," Tracy spoke to the jury.

A week had passed since Judy visited Christian and Andrew in jail.

Christian stood tall as he wore the suit that was brought to him by Andrew.

Andrew stood by his client and faced the jury.

Judy glanced at the two of them before adjusting her sportscoat.

"We have, Your Honor."

"Baliff, please retrieve the form the forewoman," Tracy enunciated.

The baliff walked over to the jury and retrieved the form.

He made eye contact with Christian as he slowly walked back to the judge. The baliff passed Tracy the form and she silently read the verdict.

Christian studied her face for any signs of the verdict but Tracy didn't show any expressions as she read the verdict.

Andrew had done digging but he hadn't found anything regarding the bodycam footage.
He had promised Christian that he wasn't going to stop searching, regardless of the verdict, and it was a promise he'd planned on keeping.
Tracy returned the form to the bailiff and he took the form back to the jury.

"Please read your verdict," she nodded her head.

The forewoman read off of the form but Christian felt as though she would pause between each word.
Beads of sweat formed on his forehead and his heart started to beat faster.
"We, the jury, find the defendant, Christian Tate…"
Christian felt as though his heart was going to beat out of his chest.
He felt as though her words were slowing to a halt as she got closer to reading the verdict.
But he continued to stand tall and didn't show any signs of weakness.

"Guilty of first-degree murder."
Several murmurs were heard around the courtroom. Christian heard a slight shriek from Keisha.
Christian felt his legs weaken but remained on his feet. Andrew put a hand on Christian's shoulder.
They could hear Keisha silently sobbing.

"We, the jury, find the defendant, Christian Tate, guilty of aggravated battery with a firearm; first shot."
Christian couldn't believe what he was hearing. He felt they'd presented a strong enough case to prove his innocence, but none of that mattered.
Christian wanted to shout, but he knew it wouldn't be wise to do so.

"We, the jury, find the defendant, Christian Tate, guilty of the second count aggravated battery."

Christian couldn't stand any longer.

He extended his arms and grabbed the arms of his chair before sitting down; Andrew remained on his feet and slightly shook his head.

A tear formed in Andrew's eye.

"We, the jury, find the defendant, Christian Tate, guilty on all three counts of official misconduct."

Several conversations could be heard around the courtroom; some were praising the verdict and others were criticizing the verdict.

"Order," Tracy gently spoke.

The courtroom silenced and she continued.

"May I see both attorneys at my desk?" she cleared her throat.

Judy and Andrew approached her desk.

She whispered amongst the lawyers and Christian looked back at Keisha.

He saw her makeup was now smeared from her tears. She couldn't stop crying.

Christian couldn't help but let a few tears accumulate as he saw his wife crying for his freedom.

He was glad she'd left their son with his grandma; although he was a newborn, Christian didn't wish to expose him to this.

Keisha looked up and shook her head in disbelief at Christian.

She mouthed out 'I love you' and he did the same.

Andrew returned and stood next to Christian.

"Your Honor, we would like to poll the jury," Andrew projected.

"Ladies and gentlemen, when someone is convicted by a jury trial, the convicted individual has the right to poll the jury. The reason for polling is to ensure these are the correct verdicts delivered by the jury, and to ensure there has been no coercion, promises, or bribers to sway the verdict," Tracy spoke.

The forewoman rose to her feet and polled the jury.

She asked each juror the same questions: 'were those then, and are these now your verdicts? Did you come to this verdict on your own accord; meaning, you haven't been threatened, promised, or coerced into making this decision?'.

Each of the jurors agreed that the verdicts were accurate.

"Ladies and gentlemen of the jury, the court would like to thank you for your time and service vested in this trial. Baliff, please escort these lovely men and women back to the jury room."

"All rise for the jury," the bailiff called.

Everyone rose to their feet although Christian wasn't paying much attention to what was being said.

He was still trying to wrap his mind around the verdict.

"You all may be seated," Tracy spoke.

The members of the court each took their seats.

Christian nudged Andrew lightly.

"I know," he spoke. Andrew didn't need Christian to explain why he nudged him.

15

"Damn, man," Raymond shook his head. "So what's happening now?" he asked as they ate in the cafeteria.

Christian tried to keep his mind busy since the verdict. He knew the media was running wild since the jury came back three weeks prior with a guilty verdict.

"I don't even know, man," he spoke. "My lawyer is *still* working to see what he can gather regarding the video, but it's still a toss-up. The judge said we'll reconvene on the 13th of September for sentencing. Shit," he looked at the clock on the wall, "that's roughly about a week away."

Raymond felt terrible for Christian and what was occurring. He knew for a fact that the verdict was tearing him up on the inside, although he kept his composure.

"Look man, be real with me. This place is designed to tear you down," Raymond shook his head. "It's important to have someone to talk to and be able to release the pressure. Man, I've been in here for years," Raymond explained. "Tell me what's up."

Christian sighed.

"Man, it's all bad," Christian confessed. "Every night, even before the verdict, I've been haunted by that night," he used the napkin to wipe his mouth. "Now that the verdict came back, everything has been going downhill," tears began to flow down Christian's face. "My wife is a mess and doesn't know how she's going to survive without me. She can't work right now considering she's on maternal leave and she doesn't have access to my pension because of this. I now have this label over my head that I'm a murderer. And I know that people in this jail are rejoicing over it." Raymond didn't utter a word as Christian spoke.

"I just talked to my wife yesterday and I could hear her silently sobbing. We said a prayer on the phone and everything else," Christian shook his head. "I'm holding on, but I'm not sure how much longer I can hold on."

Raymond embraced Christian.
"Bro, it's going to be okay," Raymond prayed as he embraced him. "Life is hard enough as it is as a Black man in America, but then you face this. I know the pressure you're feeling," Raymond patted Christian's back. "Shit, I imagine it must be harder for you. You're a cop, have a wife, a newborn, *and* you were only doing your job?" Raymond monitored the room as they spoke. "I feel for you."

As the two sat, they were approached by a group of inmates.
They all sat down around the table before one of them spoke.
"Christian Tate?" he asked.
Christian cleared his throat.
"I never introduced myself, but I roll with Ray. Dennis," he extended his hand for a shake.
Christian accepted the handshake.
"I brought the boys to just say that we've always been in your corner. We truly believe what occurred was justified and it's honestly fucked up what the jury came back with."
Dennis scratched the back of his head with his fingernail.

"Your lawyer tore them to bits and proved your innocent and they still come back with this bullshit verdict. Didn't you work with that prosecutor?" Dennis asked.

Christian didn't reply.
Raymond gave Dennis a certain look and Dennis slightly nodded.
The inmates all sat at the round table around Christian in silence to show support. They all bowed their heads.

Charles walked over to the group and spoke.
"Well," he started.
Christian raised his head to make eye contact with him.
"Seems like the little girl has finally got her day," he chuckled ominously.
The rest of the group raised their heads.
Christian didn't reply. He couldn't muster the energy to argue with Charles.
"Speak, Nigger," he roared at Christian when he saw Christian wasn't budging or even showing an interest in retaliating.
"You are sad," Christian spoke. "Truly, truly sad."
"Hey, at least I obey the law," he laughed. "I'm just thinking about that pretty little wife and kid of yours."
Anger started to grow inside of Christian and it was getting tough for him to maintain.
Charles could see the fury in Christian's eyes.

"I guess he needs a real man around and not a bitch-made nigger like you, so I'll let him call me 'Daddy'." Charles antagonized.
Christian leaped to his feet and pushed Charles back against the wall and kept his forearm against Charles' neck.
Raymond and his boys leapt up behind Christian and ran over to grab him.
Charles chuckled as Christian choked him.
"This rage you have," he managed to speak, "is exactly why that jury found you guilty."
Raymond and his crew grabbed Christian and pulled him off of Charles.

"He's not worth it, man," Raymond spoke as he held Christian from attacking Charles.

Charles chuckled and walked away.

Christian punched the wall and walked to the weight area.

When Christian arrived at the weight room, he looked over and saw Casey in the corner.

Casey rose to his feet and walked in Christian's direction.

As Casey got closer, he pulled out another shank and stabbed Christian in the side.

"Fuck," Christian winced as he punched Casey in the nose.

Casey fell back and Christian grabbed his side.

"This is for Benjamin," he sliced at Christian's face with the blade.

The knife cut Christian's cheek and Christian let his side go.

He punched Casey in the face once more before pulling him in. He kneed him in the groin and grabbed for the blade.

Christian grabbed the blade and tossed it across the room.

Casey laid on the floor and Christian got on his knees and put Casey in a headlock and tightened his grip as much as he could bear through the pain.

Casey gasped for air and Raymond walked into the room.

"Yo!" he shouted as he saw Christian in combat with the same man who'd attacked him.

His boys turned the corner and ran into the room.

Raymond ran in and pried Christian's arms away from Casey's neck.

Raymond saw the blood rushing from Christian's body and on his neck and shouted.

"Boss, let go!" he stressed. "You choking this man is causing you to flex and you're losing more blood."

Raymond managed to get Christian to loosen his grip and his group moved Casey.

Raymond picked Christian up and lifted him to his feet.

Christian extended his leg and kicked Casey in the head before the two were completely separated.

Christian spit at Casey and Raymond tussled to get him back over to the bench.

"Lay down, Boss," Raymond instructed him.

"The bastard," Christian breathed raggedly as he spoke.

"Don't talk," Raymond removed his shirt and applied pressure to Christian's wound. "Yo, Dennis, go get some help."

"I got you, man."

Dennis fled from the room to get assistance.

"You're gonna pull through," Raymond assured him.

***

"Judy, Your Honor," Andrew addressed as he entered her chambers.

"Andrew," Judy greeted him.

"Mr. Brownstone," she greeted him as she navigated her computer. "I'm just finalizing the ruling for Christian Tate," she spoke reluctantly.

"Stop," he interjected. "There's something that you all need to see."

"Mr. Brownstone, the case is over and the verdict has been issued."

"I know it's over, but this has been a mistrial," he explained.

"Excuse me?" Judy spoke.

Tracy looked up.

"Mr. Brownstone, I'm not willing to have the authenticity of my courtroom or judgments questioned."

Andrew pulled out a flash drive.

"And I want to file a motion to arrest the police commander for obstruction of justice," he looked at Judy.

She gave him a dirty look.

"What's this about?" Tracy inquired.

Andrew placed the flash drive on her desk.

"This drive..." he started, "Nah. I think you should have a look for yourself."

Tracy looked inquisitively at the drive and then at Andrew.

She plugged the flash drive into her computer and launched the file on the drive.

Judy looked at the video with Andrew and Tracy.

"*Miami P-D, freeze!*" she heard Christian shout over the video.

"Mr. Brownstone, I've already seen —," she spoke.

"Just watch," Andrew instructed.

She continued to watch the video with meticulous attention.

"*If you don't stop, you will be tased,*" Christian shouted over the video.

Andrew watched the video alongside Tracy and Judy.

"This is where he's running after Benjamin, although you've seen this part," he specified.

Tracy and Judy heard the taser discharge and watched him fall off of the fence.

"*Why you runnin' man?*" they heard Christian ask.

"*Fuck you, man,*" the three of them saw Benjamin start to rise to his feet.

She saw Christian's hand force Benjamin back to the ground.

She heard the chain links on the handcuffs and saw them come into view.

Although Tracy had already seen this, Andrew wanted her to watch the video to completion so she could compare the one she'd previously seen with this one.

The camera showed Benjamin jump to his feet reach around to his back pocket.

"*Drop your weapon,*" Christian spoke and Tracy saw Benjamin holding the firearm.

Benjamin returned his weapon to his waistband and started running again.

Tracy heard heavy breathing and saw Benjamin trip.

Where the video had previously gone black, it was playing all the way through.

Tracy raised her eyebrows and her eyes widened.

Judy gasped slightly.

The camera got closer to Benjamin as he laid on the ground. She could see Christian holding his firearm.

"*Do not move. Stay on your stomach with your arms extended,*" Christian shouted.

Tracy saw Benjamin turn around with the firearm aimed at Christian.

"*Drop your weapon,*" Christian shouted.

She saw Benjamin put his finger on the trigger and she saw Christian fire his weapon.

Tracy wrote down notes on her notepad as she watched the video.

The force of the shot caused Benjamin to flip over and lay on his stomach.

"*Shots fired,*" she heard Christian report over his radio.

"So this is how it actually went down," Tracy spoke as she shook her head.

"I smell obstruction of justice charges," Andrew chuckled.

The video continued to play in the background as Tracy continued to jot down notes.

"The commander has had an issue with my client, Christian Tate, ever since Christian didn't come in to celebrate the force's arrest record. My client felt as though most of the arrests were on African-Americans and so he refused to go. As a result, he had the video footage altered and cut before releasing it over to me."

Judy and Tracy both shook their heads at this information.

"In light of this new information, I have no choice but to overrule the verdict issued by the jury," she shook her head as she closed the notepad.

"I'm ordering that Christian Tate be released from jail, immediately," she ordered.

Andrew pulled out his phone and texted Keisha. A slight smile formed across his face as he returned his phone to his pocket.

Judy put her hands on her head as Tracy spoke.

"And, I'm going to get a warrant to arrest the commander for evidence tampering and obstruction of justice."

"Thank you, Your Honor," Andrew replied.

"Thank you, Your Honor," Judy spoke. "Congratulations, counselor," she started to Andrew, "looks like you've beaten me fair and square," she extended her hand for a shake.

"It wasn't easy," he chuckled as he shook her hand.

Tracy dialed the number to the prison and picked up the receiver.

"Yes, this is Judge Tracy Sinclair; I presided over the Florida v. Tate case," she started. "I'm well, how are you? That's good. I'm sitting here with Attorney Judy Lawrence and Attorney Andrew Brownstone, and some new evidence has been brought to my attention regarding the case," she paused.

Judy pulled out her phone and sent a text as Tracy spoke on the phone.

"It seems as though a key piece of evidence was tampered with. I have obtained a copy and have reviewed the original evidence, and based upon the video evidence, I am clearing Christian Tate of the charges brought against him and I'm overruling the jury's guilty verdict; all charges. I am ordering that he be released from prison, immediately" she ordered. "Also," she added a few seconds later, "I am signing a warrant for the police commander, Jon Tanner, for evidence tampering and obstruction of justice," she finished.

Andrew's smirk remained on his face as Tracy spoke.

Judy packed her items into her suitcase and Tracy gasped lightly.

"Okay. Well, keep me posted with what happens."

Tracy hung up the phone and displayed a look of concern.

"What'd they say?" Andrew asked.

After a few moments of silence, Tracy spoke.

"There's been a situation at the jail," she solemnly spoke.

Andrew raised his eyebrows.

"Tate has been stabbed in his side, near his kidney and his face was slashed. He's in serious condition, but he is alive," she concluded.

Andrew threw his sportscoat over his shoulder and headed for the door. He pulled out his phone.

Andrew got in his vehicle and called Keisha to inform her of what was going on.

"Keisha?" he answered.

"What's up, Drew?" she asked.

"Keisha, don't panic," he started. "But something has happened with Christian."

"I know," she started, "you told me the judge threw the case out based on the video."

"Nah, it's not that," Andrew responded.

Keisha stuttered as she heard the seriousness in his tone.

"Wh-What is it?" she questioned.

"Chris has been stabbed in the side and cut in the face."

Keisha immediately became weak in the knees when she heard this.

Andrew was concerned about the silence.

"You there, Keisha?" he asked as he approached the jailhouse.

"Yes, I'm here," she finally spoke. "What are they saying?" she asked.

"Well, I'm at the jailhouse now," he turned his car off after parking. "They say he's in serious condition but he's okay. I'm going to see him now, but if you can, head up here as well. Nothing would please him more than seeing your face."

"I'm going to drop Junior off at my mom's and then I'll be up there," she picked up the child. "I'm heading out now."

"Okay, cool," Andrew replied.

"Andrew, keep me posted with what's going on," Keisha added. "And tell Chris that I love him," he could hear her voice cracking.

"I'll tell him," Andrew spoke after a short pause. "See you soon, Keish," he ended the call and walked up the stairs to the jailhouse.
***

"Man, oh man," Raymond spoke to Christian.

Christian rubbed his side that was packed tightly and bandaged.

"This pain is surreal," he chuckled. "Never did I ever think any of this would ever happen; especially not to me."

"It's hard to believe it did," Raymond shook his head. "But we have to look at the positives. You're still alive to tell the story."

"Yeah, but look at me. I'm in the 'hospital' over this shit and I still have this verdict sitting over my head."

Andrew was at the jail but hadn't yet gotten to see Christian to deliver the news.

Keisha was also on her way to the jail and she was overly anxious since finding out what happened.

"Man, don't even worry. Everything will play and work itself out. You just have to have faith."

"To hell with that," Christian shook his head as he inhaled sharply at the pain he was feeling. "We have to get you talking with Andrew to get you out. If I couldn't get out of here, at least you can."

Raymond disagreed.

"Nah man, that's dead," he uttered. "It's all over," he looked at the heart monitor connected to Christian.

"Hey," Christian spoke, "as long as I have air in my lungs, it's not over. We need to get you home."

"Yeah, and what about you? You have a fucking newborn and a wife at home waiting on you," he argued. "We have to get *you* out of here."

Raymond was adamant.

"What the hell do you want me to do?" Christian asked.

"Fight!" Raymond retaliated.

He looked around and lowered his tone.

"We're going to pray on it and just pray that God gets you out of here."

"The same God that put me in here?" Christian asked. "Nah, I'm good."

"Boss, now I'm not the most religious person, but I do believe there's a higher power and He has the final say-so in everything."

Christian hung his head.

Traditionally, he wasn't negative and he tried his best to keep his hopes up.

But all hope seemed lost to Christian, especially with the verdict on his mind and he feared Christian Jr. would grow up without a father.

The nurse came into the room where Christian and Raymond sat.
"Mr. Tate, I've just received good news from upstairs."
Christian looked at Raymond and then looked at her.
Raymond raised his eyebrows and smirked.
"You have been cleared to go," she spoke.
"Go?" Christian was confused.
"From this room back to the cell?" Raymond asked.
"No," the nurse spoke. "From this jail."
"And transferred to a new facility, right?" Christian asked.
He couldn't bring himself to believe that he'd gotten a blessing especially after what he'd just said.
The nurse chuckled.

"No, silly. Free to go, as in all charges have been dropped and your name has been cleared," she ensured his bandage was tight and his abdomen was wrapped. She also checked the stitches in both his face and on his side. "Let's get you off this machine so you can get out of here. Everything seems stable; you just need to get some proper rest and to put all of this behind you," she started to take the sensors off of him and silence the alarms.

Christian felt his stomach sink as he heard the news, but it was a good feeling.
Once the nurse finished disconnecting him from the machines, she stepped out of the room to speak with the officers.

Raymond rose to his feet and clapped hands with Christian.
"I told you, man," he congratulated. "Sometimes, you just gotta ride on faith."
Christian nodded his head and spoke.
"Man, I just want to say thank you for all you've done since I've been in here."

"Look man, I'm just glad you're getting out of this joint. I told you everything would play out and the truth would be revealed."

"I know I may not be an officer anymore, but we're going to get you out of here, next," Christian assured him.

"Hey man, you enjoy your freedom," Raymond replied. "My time is coming and I'm going to be patient with it."

Two officers entered the room.

"Christian Tate," one of them started. "We're here to escort you up. The papers have been drawn up and you've been cleared of all charges against you."

Christian gave Raymond a warm embrace.

"Thanks, man," Christian spoke.

"No doubt," Raymond responded.

Christian rose to his feet and walked over to the officers.

"Let's go," they spoke.

The officers escorted Christian out of the room and Raymond followed shortly behind them.

As the officers escorted Christian upstairs, they heard enormous cheers coming from the foyer.

Christian wanted to smile, but he truly couldn't.

"Coming upstairs with Christian Tate. Requesting backup in the foyer to maintain order," one of the officers reported over his radio.

"10-4," the dispatch returned.

As the three of them passed by the sitting area, there were many officers present to control the inmates; there was a mixture of cheers and jeers as they walked past.

Christian kept his head held high and nodded at some of the inmates he'd met during his stay.

The inmates cheered louder and Christian chuckled inside.

"They seem pretty happy for a cop who put a lot of them in here, to be walking free," the officer spoke as they inched closer to the exit.

Christian didn't respond.

They walked Christian to an empty cell and gave him his clothes that he went into the jail with.

"Get changed," the second officer spoke.

Christian started to change his clothes but couldn't help but think about everything that occurred to land him in the position.

Now that he was walking free, he thought about how different things would be.

There would *always* be a set of people who would label him as a killer, although there was video evidence that proved his innocence.

He couldn't go back to his old job, and if he was able to, he would have eyes on him like a hawk.

He inhaled sharply as he took off the prison jumpsuit; the wound was still very sore and he was truly feeling the pain.

Christian managed to get his clothes on and knocked on the cell.

The officers opened the cell and walked him to the front.

They handed him a bag with his belongings and the first person he saw was Keisha.

She ran over to him and embraced him. Although pain ran through his body as the two connected, Christian smiled. If he could sit in jail for over a year, he could deal with this pain; it was nothing compared to the pain he would have felt if he couldn't hold her again.

Tears rolled down her cheeks as she kissed him.

"Baby," she cried. "I'm so glad you're alright."

"I'm fine, babe. Just in pain, but seeing you is making it go away." Christian hugged her tightly.

Andrew stood beside Christian and Keisha and let the two bask in the moment before speaking, moments later.

Andrew gave Christian a handshake and proceeded.

"Got the video," he chuckled at Christian. "Turns out the commander altered the evidence before handing it over.

"That bastard," Christian shook his head. "My boy," Christian smiled and embraced his lawyer.

Andrew composed himself after the embrace and switched subjects. "You know, reporters are out there waiting," he suggested. "What do you want to do?" he asked.

Christian sighed.

"Let's do this," he spoke.

"It's all you, man," Andrew replied. "Let me take this from you," he took Christian's bag of belongings and opened the door.

Christian squinted his eyes as he saw the sun and he heard shouting from reporters.

"On your count," Andrew spoke.

Christian didn't speak.

He inhaled the fresh air and stepped outside with his lawyer on his left and his wife on his right.

Reporters rushed him.

"Christian Tate, Christian Tate," one of the reporters shouted as she held a microphone in his face.

There were plenty of flashes from cameras and bright white lights emitted from the video cameras that were recording.

Christian stood erect as he kept his arm around Keisha. He looked at Andrew.

"Your plan, my command," Andrew spoke in a low tone.

Christian smiled at Andrew and looked at the reporter.

"How does it feel now that you're a free man? What are the first steps of freedom like?" she asked.

"It's just like any other steps I've taken in life," Christian shrugged. "Just trying to get back on track and take life day-by-day."

"It's reported that there was an attack on you just hours ago within the jail. Do you have any comments on that?" a different reporter asked as she noticed the gauze bandage on his face.

"I'll let the jail comment on that," Christian shook his head slightly.

Keisha continued to let the tears flow.

"I'm here to focus on the positives; not the negatives," he looked at Keisha and smiled. "I'm going home to my wife and son," he kissed her on the cheek.

"Mr. Tate, how does it feel to have gone through this, and is there anything you will be doing differently in the future if something arises?"

Christian looked at Andrew and then back to the reporter.

"No comment on that. Just taking it day-by-day," he answered.

"Ladies and gentlemen, we've got to keep it moving. Mr. Tate has had a long day and just wants to get home and move forward. I'm sure he's anxious to put all of this behind him," Andrew interjected.

"One final question," a reporter shouted. "You are one of the few cases in which evidence that has been presented post-trial and resulted in an overturned jury verdict. How does it feel to have had this verdict overturned? I mean, you were looking at life or the death penalty from their verdict." she asked.

Christian thought about her question.

"I have never changed my stance," he started. "I told you all from the beginning I was innocent, and I still stood tall and loved my city, even when the city didn't love me back. Even if the verdict wasn't overturned, there was no way I was going to plead guilty to this," he began.

Andrew tapped Christian's shoulder to suggest that he stop talking.

The three of them began to walk away and Christian heard a question asked that he couldn't ignore.

"How does it feel knowing that justice has been served?" the reporter shouted.

Christian stopped in his tracks and looked at the reporter in her eyes.

"Justice?" he started. "When a police commander lies on you and alters evidence to lock you away, and then his brother gives you hell while you're on the inside, all because you all didn't agree on policing, that's not justice," Christian spoke. "When you get called racial slurs and tormented by those who have been sworn to serve and protect, that's not justice." A tear came to Christian's eye.

Keisha put her hand on his chest.

"And when you're a Black man or woman, and the police stop, frisk, assault, arrest, and sometimes shoot and kill you for no other reason than you're Black and they see black as a threat, that's not justice," he continued.

Christian sighed.

"Caucasian officers go day-by-day getting off on harassing Black people. And what happens to them? Administrative leave, suspension with pay, desk jobs; hell, some even get to go right back on duty because the law calls it justified," Christian rolled his eyes slightly and saw Andrew standing at his side. "But here I am, a Black cop, and I shoot a White boy after it's been proven that he had a firearm and pulled it on me. Immediately, I am stripped of my job, my rights, and everything I've done for this city goes down the drain," he shook his head and held Keisha tighter.

"Although I walk free today, it is solely because my distinguished lawyer here," he looked at Andrew, "worked hard to obtain the unaltered evidence to clear my name. This isn't justice. This is America."

***

\

www.ingramcontent.com/pod-product-compliance
Lightning Source LLC
Chambersburg PA
CBHW032014240626
47153CB00003B/1247